Brand's gray eyes burned into Fliss

"By the way, I forgot to do the dishes last night. Do them, will you—please?"

Last night she'd have done them—if not happily, willingly enough. Particularly, crazy as it seemed now, if Brand had been beside her helping. To kill the sudden pain of that mental picture, she yelled, "No, I won't," and then snatched up the dish of rolls and cassava cakes, and threw it across the table toward him.

As it hurtled past Brand's ear, he got to his feet. "That was a pretty infantile thing to do," he said at last.

"You know something, Brand Carradine? I hate you—I really hate you."

He gave her one brief glinting glance. "I can live with that."

REBECCA KING

dark guardian

Harlequin Books

TORONTO • NEW YORK • LONDON
AMSTERDAM • PARIS • SYDNEY • HAMBURG
STOCKHOLM • ATHENS • TOKYO • MILAN
MADRID • WARSAW • BUDAPEST • AUCKLAND

Harlequin Presents first edition July 1992
ISBN 0-373-11477-X

Original hardcover edition published in 1991
by Mills & Boon Limited

DARK GUARDIAN

CHAPTER ONE

SOMBRA?

Fliss's fingers closed convulsively on the scrap of paper, crumpling it then dropping it on to the sand.

'What did you draw, then, Fliss?'

Several pairs of eyes were watching her with avid curiosity, and somehow she had to pull herself together.

'Oh—Sombra,' she said carelessly, but knew that there was a tremor in her voice. 'I have to get some ornament from beside the swimming-pool.'

One of the girls, propped up against the trunk of a palm tree, whistled. 'Wow! Whoever thought that one up?' she asked innocently.

Who indeed? thought Fliss grimly. However had she got herself mixed up in this latest game of dares? If she'd just turned up tonight, instead of joining the group lounging in the afternoon sun devising the list of 'trophies' each had to produce at the beach party that night, she wouldn't have found herself in this mess.

Sombra. Grampy had told her that that meant shadow. What a fitting name for the secluded villa, perched on that lonely headland jutting out into the Caribbean and hidden among the overgrown bushes and poinciana trees. She hated the place even in daylight—it had always given her the creeps, like something out of a seedy horror movie. . .

As the slight tremor ran through her she realised that one of the boys, sprawled alongside her, was idly tracing a dried palm frond around the outline of the small, heart-shaped birthmark of pale skin on her upper thigh. She edged away.

'And that new tenant. . .' Behind the haze of sweet-smelling cigarette smoke the girl rolled her eyes. . .'oh, boy.'

'But have you seen him, Loretta?' One of the other girls stopped preening herself in her hand-mirror and sat bolt upright. 'I thought he was some kind of crazy recluse or something, never setting foot outside the place.'

'Oh, yes, I've seen him all right. He came into our store the other day ordering provisions—liquor mainly.'

'But what's he *like*?' persisted the other.

'Well—you know.' She slanted a tantalising cat's smile at their expectant faces. 'Six feet plus, black hair, grey eyes, and——'

'And. . .?'

'He looks,' the girl frowned reflectively, 'kind of *dangerous*.' A faintly lascivious smirk flicked across her face, but then she turned to Fliss, who had felt herself growing steadily paler beneath her suntan. 'What's the matter? Not chicken, are you? Hey folks, the baby's chicken.'

'Me, chicken?' Fliss brushed away some of the fine white sand which was sticking to her bare stomach and lay back carelessly on her beach towel. 'You must be joking. I'll go as soon as it gets dark.'

'Hmm. I'll swap dares with you, if you like. After all, a babe in arms like you wouldn't know what to do with a hunk like that.'

For a split second Fliss hesitated but then caught the challenging spark of malice in the other girl's dark eyes. For weeks now, ever since she'd drifted in with this crowd, Loretta in particular had been probing, trying to wheedle out of her the extent—or, rather, the lack—of her sexual experience, and she didn't intend to give her any clues now.

She managed a cool smile. 'No, thanks. The hunkier the better. But in any case, I don't intend for him to catch me.' And, tossing back her heavy blonde hair, she leapt to her feet, ran down the beach and hurled herself into the warm, milky green shallows.

She swam away from the shore with powerful strokes in an effort not only to free herself of the unpleasant taste of Loretta in her mouth, but also to escape from those strange tensions which for days had been coiling inside her.

Then, when she finally tired, she turned on to her back and floated, her hair spreading like a fan behind her, her body before her, the brief turquoise bikini emphasising rather than concealing her high, full breasts, the rounded, womanly curves of her hips. Those silky sweeps of golden tanned flesh. . .

As the peculiar, half-conscious feelings began yet again to tug unnervingly at her mind, she turned her head away to gaze at the horizon, the shore—anywhere than at the frightening voluptuousness of her own body.

Beside her a shoal of small silver fish had been flitting to and fro, but now, as she floated motionless in the swell, some of them ventured nearer and began nibbling gently at her. Their tiny mouths barely stirred the fine sunbleached hairs on her skin and yet, as they grazed at her sides and thighs, an even more disturbing sensation, like a tiny electric current, ran prickling through her whole body from each minute point of contact. It aroused in her a feeling of intense pleasure, but at the same time intense unease, as though all the breath in her body were suspended and she hung weightless between the sky and the sea.

'Hi, Fliss.' One of the boys surfaced beside her and the fish were gone in a flick of silver lightning.

As he floated alongside her, he said casually, 'I was thinking; if you're really uptight about Sombra, not that I'm saying you are, of course——' as she scowled at him '——I don't mind changing with you.'

'Oh, thanks, Scott.' She smiled. Unlike some of the others, he was really rather a sweetie under the big macho act that all the boys affected. 'You mean you'll let me steal the Admiral Rodney pub sign instead, and have Carl Henriques chasing me all over Kingston? No, thanks. I'll take my chance with Loretta's hunk.'

'Well,' he winked at her, 'you don't know this, of course, but he——' He broke off teasingly.

'W-what about him?' she asked in trepidation.

'He's off the island. I saw him at the airport this morning. He was catching the Miami flight.'

Relief surged through her. So all she had to do was

brave the terrors of the house, not of the unknown man as well.

'Oh, thanks a million, Scott.'

'Any time, Flissie. You can give me my reward at the party tonight.'

'Well.' She smiled uncertainly. 'That depends.'

'You're not going out again this evening are you, Felicia?'

As she came out on to the veranda, her grandfather glanced up over his spectacles at her, taking in her black cotton jersey T-shirt dress and swept-up hair, then very carefully set down the old, dog-eared book he was reading.

'Now, Grampy.' She wagged a playful finger at him. 'You know I told you Morris is having a barbecue at their beach house. I must go—all the gang will be there.'

'But will his parents be there?' He gazed anxiously up at her.

'Well,' she hesitated, 'no, they won't. But don't worry—I'm not a baby. I'm seventeen.'

'But that set you've got in with. . . I've heard some of them have been in trouble—stealing and drugs.'

'Grampy.' She dropped down beside his chair, putting her arm round his thin shoulders. 'I swear to you I would never take drugs or——' she bit her lip as she thought of what she was about to do, then added vehemently, '—never.'

'But they're older than you, and they're all so wild.'

'Well, you're always telling me I'm wild.'

But he did not respond to her playful tone. 'And so you are, my darling child.' He sighed heavily. 'I do wonder whether, when your mother died and. . .'

Their eyes met and slid away. 'And when Daddy married again and didn't want me any more,' she said in a cold little voice, still not proof against the pain of that seven-year-old memory.

'Oh, don't say that, love.'

'Why not? It's the truth.'

He took her hands in his. 'Well, whatever happened then, you know you're everything to me, don't you?' She nodded, her eyes misty. 'But I do ask myself whether I shouldn't have come back to England to raise you, instead of having you brought out here to me.'

'Oh, no.' She was horrified. 'Growing up here in Jamaica with you,' her eyes wandered around the veranda, coating the shabby bamboo furniture and peeling green paint on the louvres with a shining layer of love, 'has been wonderful. Besides,' she gave him a teasing smile, 'how could you ever have borne to be dragged away from your beloved old coral?'

She looked up at him with a sudden spurt of pride. She had never really got used to the fact that Grampy was, to outsiders, the great J. G. Sinclair, a world authority on the corals of the Caribbean whose book on the reefs around Jamaica was still regarded, even thirty years after it had been published, as *the* last word on the subject.

But he was not to be distracted. 'Mmm. But perhaps if we'd been there, well—they say the tropics mature young English girls too quickly. Out here you've become a woman suddenly, without your blind old grandfather noticing,' he gave her a sad little smile, 'while inside you're still a child.'

'Oh, but I'm not, Grampy,' she said indignantly. 'I'm really grown up. You know Mother Superior hasn't put me in detention once this week. She told me only yesterday,' her voice dropped several octaves and she struck a dramatic pose, ' "Felicia Naughton, you have more than your share of the devil in you, but I have hope for you yet." '

He laughed indulgently. 'My darling child, you are incorrigible. What am I going to do with you?'

'And what am *I* going to do with *you*?' She rumpled his hair, then leapt to her feet.

'But you're surely not going yet?'

She looked down, veiling her sapphire eyes with long lashes to hide the guilt. 'Y-yes, I must. I promised Morris I'd help get the barbecue ready. Now, you're not to worry. I promise I shan't be late.' And, dropping a kiss on the furrow between his brows, she fled.

Once at the bottom of the driveway, though, she turned the front wheel of her moped not downhill towards town and the beach, but up the lane which led through the fields of sugar-cane, over the hill, then freewheeled down towards the dark headland which she could glimpse ahead, black against the dull basalt of the sea.

The dry stems of cane rustled in the night breeze, sounding like a tiny, unpleasant whisper in her ear, and she was almost relieved when she saw the grey stone gate-posts and the white board, proclaiming in harsh black letters, 'Sombra'.

Leaving the moped out of sight behind a clump of bamboo and hitching the skirt of her dress back down, she set off along the drive. The moon was behind a bank of cloud and from all around her in the darkness came tiny sounds—creatures that she could not see but which were watching her—so that her mouth ran dry with fear. To try and blot out those covert noises she started running, until all she could hear was the sound of her own laboured breathing.

Ahead of her as she broke from the shelter of the trees was Sombra. The house lay wrapped in darkness; not a light showed from any of the rooms. Well, that was a relief; she'd been more than half afraid that one of the permanent servants would be there. But, she told herself now, with the tenant safely away in Miami no self-respecting servant was going to be sitting around here when he could be living it up in Kingston.

Just then, though, from somewhere a dog barked and she tensed again, the hairs on her neck prickling. Many of the houses on the island, particularly the more isolated ones, kept at least one of what the locals called 'bad dogs'—creatures that would take your leg off at the knee as soon as growl at you. But the bark had been a distant one and Fliss allowed herself very slightly to relax once more.

She stood a moment longer, gazing into the darkness, trying to get her bearings. There was no sign of a swimming-pool, but it was probably at the rear of the house. She drew a deep breath and then, even though there was no one about, found herself slipping off her flat sandals before scampering across the expanse of coarse lawn and up the bank to one side of the silent house.

Yes, here it was—a large oval expanse of water, the surface as unruffled as black satin, while at the far end a group of latticed sun-loungers was just visible in the even darker shadows beneath an old poinciana tree.

But where was the ornament, this shell that she had to bring away with her? She walked a few paces along the tiled edge of the pool, peering around her, then gave a hastily stifled groan of disbelief. There, surely, was the faint outline of a statue—a water nymph perhaps. And yes—yes, she was holding in one hand a shape, rounded like a conch shell, which glinted softly through the darkness. But what no one had told her—least of all Loretta—was that the figure was perched not at the side of the pool, as she'd fondly imagined, but way out of reach in the very centre.

'Oh, *damn*!' She stared across the gulf of uninviting water, tapping one foot against a tile. Even now, it wasn't too late. She could say that the statue wasn't there, that the new tenant must have moved it, or that the shell was broken. Come to that, she didn't even have to go to the stupid party, did she? Oh, yes, and have Loretta, Scott—everyone—call her chicken?

No. She'd just have to hitch up her dress, wade in and get the wretched thing. But how deep was the pool in the centre? How would she be able to explain to Grampy going home in soaking wet clothes? He already thought the parties she'd been going to lately were wild enough, without that.

With a last swift glance at the silent house, she let go of her sandals, unzipped the back of her dress and wriggled it down over her hips. She kicked it away from her then slid off her cotton panties and dropped them on to the dress.

Just for a moment she hesitated, listening. Everywhere remained perfectly quiet and yet, unaccountably, she suddenly found herself shivering violently. Ugh. Someone walking over my grave, she thought, or maybe it was the delayed effects of that slug of white rum—the main item of what Grampy grandly called his drinks cabinet—that she'd helped herself to before setting out, in a vain attempt to calm her twanging nerves.

But then, not giving herself the chance of any more delay, she lowered herself into the pool. With only the tiniest gasp as her hot skin met the cool, silken water, she struck out for the centre where, treading water, she clutched first at the plinth which supported the statue, then at the nymph itself.

'Ooops—sorry,' she said to the unseeing face, as her fingers brushed across the curve of a stone breast. If the gang could see me now, she thought. She broke into a high-pitched giggle which seemed to bounce back at her from around the pool, and even after she bit her lip, instantly suppressing the sound, it went on inside her head as a faint, surreptitious echo.

You know something, I think you're a touch light-headed, my girl; that rum was definitely not a good idea, she told herself sternly as her wet fingers grappled ineffectually with the shell. But then, suddenly, it came away from the encircling stone arm.

'Got it!' With a tiny hiss of triumph she held it up for a moment, its crystalline curves gleaming softly, then holding it very carefully above the water in one hand she dog-paddled to the pool edge.

It really was blissful here: the blue-black tropical sky overhead, the night scents from the shrubs and trees, the sensual touch of silky water against her bare flesh. A thrill of illicit delight ran through her. Perhaps she'd stay here a little longer, luxuriating in a few secret, stolen minutes swimming, with only that beautiful sea nymph for company. She'd just put the fragile shell safely down on the grass and——

A cry of sheer, heart-stopping terror was wrenched from her as, hauling herself out of the pool, she made contact with a pair of legs. As she tried to scramble to her feet, her one coherent thought now to escape, the shell slipped from her grasp and, beyond the periphery of her fear, she heard it splash back into the water.

Next moment, a hand had seized her roughly by the arm.

'Dive for it.' The man's voice was harsh with anger.

'No, please. I'm sorry——' she began, then too late clutched at the pool edge as he pushed her and she felt herself fall helplessly backwards.

She surfaced coughing and choking for air, her hair plastered over her face so that she could scarcely see.

The man, a darkly threatening shadow, was towering over her. So at least one of the servants had stayed here, keeping guard. But no. His accent had been English—he must be the new tenant. Scott had been dreadfully wrong.

Fliss, almost sinking under the weight of her fear, looked up at him helplessly. Suppose she swam to the far end of the pool. . .? But, even as she half turned, he took a couple of warning steps along the side.

She'd be expelled for this, and what would Grampy say then? She bit on her mouth as scalding tears blurred her eyes.

'Dive, damn you,' the man snarled.

Perhaps if she retrieved the hateful shell he'd then let her go. Taking a deep breath, she dived down into the inky depths, her fingers groping frenziedly until red stars reeled through her brain and she was forced upward.

She trod water, gulping in the oxygen, as he stared down implacably at her, something in the immobility of that black outline chilling her even more. She shivered, then dived again, and this time her hands found what they were seeking and, weak with relief, she came up again, clutching the shell.

She set it on the edge of the pool at his feet, a gesture almost as though she were a supplicant kneeling before some pagan deity. But there was no mercy in this particular god. As she clambered out, barely even aware now that she was naked, and uncaring anyway in her desperate need to escape, he grabbed her by the arm.

'L-let me go, please.' Her voice, always low, came out as a husky, terrified whisper.

'Oh, not just yet.' His fingers tightened as she cringed away, and through the intense darkness they stared at each other. 'I don't let thieves get off that easily.'

Through all the fear, his words stung her on the quick. 'I'm not a thief,' she muttered.

'No?' The voice, icy with contempt, flayed her but she threw back her head proudly.

'No, I'm not. If you'll just let me explain——'

But his fingers tightened even more on her wrist, tugging her along behind him.

'Over here, where I can get some lights on.'

'No—*please.*'

As Fliss began to struggle frantically, her wet feet slipped on the tiles. She almost overbalanced into the pool behind her, taking the man with her, but he braced himself and, pulling her into his arms, steadied her.

Somewhere beyond the explosive clamour of her heartbeats, she heard a hissed intake of breath as he realised that she was naked, and for a second he stilled, so that under her right shoulder-blade she felt the violent thump of his heart. She had to keep struggling, but something was rooting her to the spot, making her limbs heavy, and as though taking her stillness for acquiescence he tilted her face towards him and brought his mouth down on hers.

Fliss had been kissed before—clumsy, boyish kisses from which she would surreptitiously slide away. This was different, as wine and water, sun and moon, love and hate were different. Under the gently insistent pressure of his lips she opened hers and felt his tongue slide between them to feed on the honeyed sweetness of her mouth.

When she brought up her hands in fluttering protest, he caught both her wrists with his free hand, splaying her fingers against his chest so that through the thin, silky material of the wrap he was wearing she felt the fiery heat of his body. Before she could draw back, it had leapt through her fingertips, like a forest inferno clearing a fire break, and run through her own body, the flames licking at her, bringing to life emotions which until then had barely existed.

His mouth was sucking her whole being out of her body in wild response to him. All thoughts of right and wrong suspended, she reeled against him for support and felt him lift her into his arms to swing her across the damp tiles of the pool surround. He lowered her on to the grass and, without releasing her mouth, brought his weight against her, so that together they slipped to their knees.

He laid her down, the coarse grass scratching at her back and legs, and then she heard him pull open the tie of his wrap. At that same moment, the moon emerged from behind the clouds and, looking up, she could make out the silhouette of his body—the body, it seemed to her now, that she had seen for months in her half-girl, half-woman dreams. And then he came down beside her.

As though still gripped by those dreams, she felt his hands cup her full ripe breasts, his teeth suckling gently at them until they strained against him and she gasped aloud at the sharp stab of pleasure-pain which shot through her whole frame.

He put his hands beneath her waist and lifted her to his mouth, his tongue and lips trailing erotic patterns across the damp flesh of her stomach. Her eyes gazed unseeing at the night sky and she trembled under him, her fingers twining and gripping convulsively in his thick, springy hair. With the very edge of her consciousness, she heard him mutter something against her skin; then he raised himself and came down on her, blotting out the stars, the night, everything.

Just once she bit on the soft inner flesh of her mouth, as a searing pain split her in two, and then he was past the fragile barrier and taking full possession of her, the pulsating force building at once into a driving rhythm which carried her with it, far from her own being to somewhere very distant outside of herself. She cried out and a shudder ran through her as the blossoms of a million flowers sprang up inside her, and then a trillion petals came softly drifting back to earth, burying her in their scented weight. . .

Fliss stirred and opened her eyes. The moon was still out and its serene, untroubled face was gazing down on the aftermath of the scene which had been played out in the warm, tropical darkness below. For a moment she lay uncomprehending, then the rough grass beneath her aching body brought her to the stark realisation of where she was—and of what she had done.

Sick now with fear, and shame, she rolled over. He

was lying a few feet away from her, half on his side, one arm pillowing his head. In the intense shadow cast by that arm his face was invisible, but the moonlight silvered his body, touching every hard line, transforming him into a beautiful classical sculpture.

She rolled hastily away, huddling into a ball, the back of one hand pressed to her mouth. What had she done? She began very slightly to tremble, and the trembling increased until her whole body was shivering so violently that her teeth chattered.

His hand reached out and gently touched her on her shoulder. 'You're cold.'

A moment later, she felt herself enfolded in his silky wrap, but still the dreadful shivering would not stop, and he said, 'I'll fetch you a sweater.'

She heard his footsteps retreat, then a light went on in the house and a yellow oblong fell across the pool. Scrambling shakily to her feet, she found her clothes, snatched them up and ran across the lawn, forcing her legs which turned to rubber under her.

In her terror of being caught, she turned off from the winding drive, fighting her way through bushes which clawed at her face and body, to emerge by her moped. Somehow she fumbled herself into her dress, then leaned against the bank, her head in her hands, running her trembling fingers through her damp hair.

And then they stilled. Her left earring—it was gone, ripped off in that last crazy skelter through the undergrowth. Those earrings: amethyst set in gold, shaped like tiny humming-birds. They were her most precious possession, her present from Grampy on her birthday last year, and now one was gone.

She gave a little whimper of misery but then climbed on to her moped and, half blinded by the tears which were streaming down her cheeks, rode away.

'I'm home, Grampy.'

Fliss trudged up the steps, dumped her school books tied together by their strap down on the front porch, and stood listening, but her grandfather did not call back.

He must be out for once. Good—that meant she could slink unnoticed to her room. She'd have a long, cool shower; maybe that would buck her up, for the heat had really been getting to her the last few days, so that she'd been listless and dispirited. Sister Stella Clare had even looked hard at her that morning in class and, with a slight softening of her usual caustic tone, remarked that she hoped Felicia wasn't sickening for something—she'd been preternaturally quiet for far too long.

Perhaps she really was ill, she thought hopefully— she certainly couldn't sleep. Every night she tossed fretfully in between dark, troubled dreams which, by the time she woke, trembling, had vanished until the next time. Oh, don't kid yourself, she told herself savagely. What's wrong with you is the aftershock of that night. Had it only been a week ago, that cataclysmic encounter at Sombra, when harsh reality had so brutally broken through her flimsy fantasy world?

But at least she wasn't pregnant. She felt again the lurch of joyous relief which had liberated her from that particular nightmare. How would she ever have borne that—to be pregnant by a total stranger, a man she was never going to meet again? Even so, that heavy knot of misery and guilt in her chest was still weighing her down to the ground.

As she went towards the green swing-door, Maybelle, her grandfather's elderly housekeeper, came out.

'So there you are, Miss Felicia.' She scrutinised the girl, until Fliss shifted uncomfortably. 'You very peaky. You sickening for something?'

Oh, no, not another one. 'I'm fine.' Fliss produced what she hoped was a reassuring smile. 'Is Grampy out?'

'No, he's on the back veranda.' Her voice dropped. 'He got a visitor—a man.'

She groaned inwardly. 'Who?'

The housekeeper shrugged. 'I don't know. They're talking about coral.'

Fliss groaned again, this time out loud. Yet another in the seemingly endless line of tourists who, having discovered the whereabouts of the great J. G. Sinclair, had come to give Grampy the benefit of everything they knew—or, more usually, didn't know—about the coral reefs that lay off the island. Well, she'd just put in a token appearance, then go and have that shower.

The two men were deep in conversation as she went through to the veranda. She heard first her grandfather's soft tones, then in reply another voice—a voice that, surely, she recognised; a voice that she had heard just a few nights earlier in the darkness by that pool at Sombra!

The visitor was sitting with his back to her in one

of the tall basket chairs. All she could see of him was one tanned arm, which hung negligently over the side, and a thatch of thick black hair. It couldn't be *him*. It mustn't be.

'Ah, there you are, my sweet.' Her grandfather turned to her as she hovered uncertainly in the doorway.

'H-hello, Grampy,' she stammered.

'Come and sit down, my dear.'

She hesitated but then, driven by the need to be certain, somehow propelled her legs past the man, without a glance in his direction, and dropped down by her grandfather's chair. She leaned across and kissed him on the forehead, keeping her face averted for a few moments more as she struggled for composure.

'Felicia, this is Mr Carradine—Brandon Carradine, I think you said?'

'That's right, sir. But please, call me Brand.'

Fliss flinched inwardly. There could be no doubt now. That deep, dark voice, the harsh sardonic edge subdued now under a veneer of social politeness but lurking still not far beneath the surface. . .

'Brand, let me introduce my only granddaughter, Felicia.'

By a supreme effort of will, she managed to raise her eyes to him, but instead of the start of recognition darkening those eyes—Loretta had been right, she thought involuntarily; they were grey, a pale, almost silvery grey—which she had braced herself to face, there was the briefest nod, a formal, 'Felicia,' and an instant return to the beautiful water-colour draw-ings—the originals of the illustrations of Grampy's book—that were spread out on the low table before him.

'These really are superb—quite superb,' he mur-mured. 'The reproductions just don't do them justice. This staghorn, for instance.' With great care, he picked up one of the sheets. 'You've caught its fragile delicacy exactly, far more than any photograph could.'

Fliss sank back on her heels, weak relief washing through her, and yet, foolishly, also a slight pique. How could he not recognise her? But then she looked down at herself and thought ironically, very easily. After all, she was wearing surely the best disguise ever invented. Just for once, she could have kissed every bit of that loathsome school uniform—the shapeless royal blue gymslip, the blue and white gingham blouse, the prissy blue tie, the straw boater, to be worn level over the forehead, and best of all the two fat blonde pigtails which hung down her back.

She was perfectly safe, and they were so engrossed in their conversation that she could easily slip away unnoticed; but something—a curiosity, perhaps, to watch this man, sitting here, quite unaware, in this so different, so *civilised* setting—made her, instead, lean back on a cushion, her elbow propped on her grandfather's chair, and regard Brand Carradine steadily from under the brim of her straw hat.

What had Loretta said about him? 'He looks kind of *dangerous*.' Was this the face of a dangerous man? With a little ripple of that same fear she'd felt a week ago, Fliss decided that it was—very much so. It was a lean face, the cheekbones sharp under the tanned skin, the lips thin, as though from habitually being held taut, yet delicately drawn. Not a conventionally handsome face, but there was—*something* in it. Maybe it was those beautiful eyes, veiled now by long black lashes as he glanced down at the sheaf of drawings, flicking through them with lean, sensitive-looking fingers. Those fingers which had, with such lethal delicacy, roused in her emotions which——

As though sensing her eyes on him, he glanced up, meeting her gaze. Instantly she blushed rose-red and looked hastily away.

'Well, there are several good real estate people in town.' Her grandfather was clearly reverting to the conversation she must have interrupted, and Fliss stiffened. Real estate! Did that mean that Brand Carradine was aiming to buy a property; settle here instead of just being a short-term tenant? 'But for what you're looking for, you might do better in the States.'

'I made a quick trip up to Miami last week—there and back in the day,' Fliss forced her eyes to remain fixed on the knot in the wooden floorboard at her feet, 'and picked up details of a couple of places that might be worth looking at. But I'll take my time, and I'd be glad of any advice you can give me before I buy.'

Fliss shifted uncomfortably and her grandfather turned to her. 'I'm sorry, my dear, we're ignoring you.' She murmured something, happy to remain unnoticed, but he went on, 'Do you have children, Brand?'

'No.' The word came swift and curt.

'In that case you probably don't realise how quickly they grow up.' Fliss winced inwardly as he took hold of one of her pigtails. 'It's only a year or so ago that I wouldn't let her cut her lovely hair, so what does she do? Chop off one plait—so then of course she had to have the rest off.' Over her bent head, she sensed the two men exchange indulgent smiles. 'I think she really ought to go back to England to school now she's seventeen. What do you think, Brand?'

Oh, don't ask *his* opinion as to my welfare—please.

Carradine's gaze flicked over her briefly. 'Well, perhaps you're right. Boarding-school certainly did me good—knocked the devil out of me.'

Something in his tone, the patronising way he had dismissed her, added to her earlier pique. All she had to do, she thought resentfully, was leap to her feet and denounce him for what he'd done to her. He'd be off this veranda—and most likely the island too—before he knew what had hit him.

But all she said was, 'Are you so sure of that, Mr Carradine?' She stood up. 'If you'll excuse me, Grampy, I want to start my homework before dinner.'

And, with a cool nod at the other man, she walked into the house, very dignified.

Once in her bedroom, though, she realised that she was trembling in every limb, as though from fever. She stood in the middle of the room, breathing deeply as if she had just emerged from a storm-tossed sea. Struggling to regain normality, she forced herself to arrange her books on her work table and pulled up a chair. But it was no use—she just couldn't settle to her work yet; not while she could still hear that deep voice drifting in through the half-closed louvres.

Perhaps she'd better have that shower first. Shedding her uniform, leaving it in an untidy heap on the bed, she went through to the adjoining bathroom and stepped into the shower cubicle, where she stood letting the cool, refreshing water flow over her for several minutes.

As she began towelling herself dry, she caught sight of her reflection in the bathroom mirror and paused, studying herself critically. Beneath the suntan, her face was a pale oval, the delicate bone-structure sharpened by sleepless nights and now—even more— by the shock of coming face to face with Brand Carradine again. There were dark smudges beneath her sapphire eyes, while her wide, full mouth was drawn tight with tension.

And her body—her eyes strayed downwards over the ripe fullness of her breasts, and beyond. . . What was it Grampy had said, just before she'd set out for Sombra half a lifetime ago? You've become a woman suddenly, while inside you're still a child. She screwed up her face as though from a physical blow, then turned abruptly from the mirror and went back into the bedroom.

But she knew instinctively that there was still no point in trying to get down to her work. She would just sit, staring unseeingly at her books, as she had done each evening this week. She had to take a hold of herself, shake herself out of this state. Something physical—a swim, perhaps. Yes, surely that would do it.

She just hoped that none of the gang would be at the beach. She hadn't gone to the party with them that night, of course—instead, she'd crept into the house, called out falteringly, 'I'm back, Grampy. I'm tired so I'm off to bed,' and fled to the sanctuary of her room before he could come out into the hall to greet her—and she'd avoided them ever since, past caring what they would make of her sudden disappearing act. . .

The voices had faded from the veranda, so Carradine had probably left. But she didn't want to risk another encounter, so, slipping on her turquoise bikini, she snatched up her towelling beach robe and ran lightly along the passage and out through the front mesh door—just in time to cannon into him as he mounted the steps from the garden.

She must have caught him off balance for he nearly fell backwards, and she put out an instinctive hand to steady him.

'Sorry!'

'Really, my dear,' remonstrated her grandfather, 'you're always in such a hurry.'

'Yes, I know, Grampy. Be back soon.' She dropped a kiss on his cheek, threw an apologetic grimace in Carradine's direction, and scurried on down the steps.

As she paused at the bottom to put on her beach wrap, she heard her grandfather say concernedly, 'Are you all right, Brand? Come and sit down again and I'll get you a drink.'

'No, no, I'm fine.' But his voice was rough. 'It's this humidity—I'm not really acclimatised yet. . .'

* * *

When Fliss got back, her grandfather was sitting on the veranda—alone, her quick glance registered with relief.

'I'll just change for dinner,' she said.

'All right, dear. But before you do—Inspector Graham from the Kingston Police phoned while you were out.'

'Oh?' Her stomach lurched violently down past her knees.

'He asked if you'd ring him back at the station.'

She swallowed, but then, seeing the apprehension in his eyes, forced what she hoped was a reassuring grin. 'I expect he's found out I didn't do my maths homework last night.'

When she trailed slowly back out, it was almost dark. From the depths of the garden, a glow-worm was blinking green fire at her.

'Well?'

'Oh, nothing much.' She shrugged, not meeting his gaze. 'S-some things were stolen in Kingston at the weekend and there have been complaints, so the police. . .' Her voice trailed away miserably.

'You weren't involved, were you?' Alarm sharpened his voice.

'No—no, of course not.' She knelt down and put her arms around him. 'Oh, Grampy, you're right. I don't want to stay here. I want to go back to England.'

And, as she laid her head on his shoulder, the unhappiness which had simmered within her for the past week broke out into loud, rending sobs.

CHAPTER TWO

FLISS curled up by the gas fire, tucking her toes under her, way out of any draughts. Her two flat-mates were both going out and she was looking forward to an evening alone. She liked both Deb and Lizzie, and had been grateful for the chance to share with them, but she was always slightly conscious that she was the 'Third Girl'—if only because they were several years older and aeons more street-wise than she was.

Besides, even after nearly four years in London, she'd never quite got used to always having people around her. So, a few hours on her own—bliss.

'By the way,' Deb, her red hair bristling with rollers, appeared in the doorway, 'how did it go today?'

'The audition, you mean?' Fliss said reluctantly.

'What else?' The other girl eyed her. 'You blew it, didn't you? You know something, Fliss? You really are some crazy girl. Here you are, with the kind of looks and figure that would make any producer shout Alleluia, and what do you do? Turn up, every time, in baggy old flying suits, that gorgeous hair of yours gelled down, and those ghastly wrap-around sunglasses that you practically sleep in. Just what are you trying to prove, for heaven's sake?' Shaking her head, Deb expelled her breath in disgust.

'I know.' And Fliss also knew that she sounded

defensive. 'But if I'm going to get any decent parts, it's going to be because of my acting ability.'

'Yes, but you——' the older girl burst out exasperatedly, then stopped abruptly.

'—haven't got any. Well, not enough, anyway,' Fliss completed for her with a faint smile.

'No, I wasn't going to say that,' Deb protested hotly.

'Maybe not—but that's the way it's beginning to look.'

And it was. Since finishing her drama course, apart from a couple of walk-on appearances in a new soap that had sunk without leaving the slightest suds behind it, the acting roles had been non-existent, and Fliss was rapidly losing all faith in her ability to break through.

The one thing she was absolutely sure about was that she was going to survive—or go under—without drawing on Grampy's meagre financial resources. He'd insisted on coming with her to England and making a home for her through her schooling and then the drama course, but had finally, a year ago, been forced to accept that the damp climate was undermining his health and returned to Jamaica.

Through optimistic letters and phone calls, she had done her best to persuade him how well things were going, but, when she'd gone back to the island for Christmas, he'd looked far from convinced.

'Oh, well, Deb,' she said with forced cheerfulness, 'it's back to wrinkled hands doing the washing-up at Leoni's, I suppose.'

The telephone shrilled outside in the tiny hall and

a bedroom door opened and banged to as Lizzie flew through to answer it.

'Oh, hi, Al.'

Al. The boss of that kissogram firm she worked for evenings. Deb rolled her eyes expressively and went back to her room.

'Of course I can't.' Lizzie's voice rose shrilly. 'You *know* I'm due at that Islington pub at seven as Sexy Little Nurse, and then I've got to do my Me-Jane you-Tarzan bit out at Hounslow, so how the hell do you think I can be up West for eight. . .? No, I don't know—hang on a sec.'

Her elfin face appeared in the doorway. 'Doing anything tonight, Fliss?'

'Well, I——'

'Great. Look, do me a favour, sweetie, will you? Al wants me to fit in another job—in the West End—but I'll never make it in time.'

'Oh, no. I couldn't.' Fliss shrank back, horrified.

'Oh, come on, pet.' Lizzie sat herself on the arm of the chair. 'Vicky and Karen are both ill, and he's going bananas. The money's good,' she added enticingly.

'I'd really rather not.' Fliss looked up at her earnestly.

'Why not, for God's sake? There's nothing to it.'

Fliss bit her lip. Impossible to explain, without sounding horribly priggish, that while most kissogram firms were thoroughly respectable, she'd never liked the look of the rather flash Al—and certainly not the way he'd looked at her, on the occasions when he'd called at the flat to take Lizzie on one of her assignments. But it was more than that. Men found her highly attractive, she couldn't escape that fact, but for over four years now she'd managed to avoid the remotest physical involvement. And now, to flaunt her body for a roomful of them—she went hot at the thought.

'Perhaps Deb——' she began hopefully.

'And snarl up her first date with that fancy stock-broker she's been angling for for weeks? I don't think so. Oh, *please*, Fliss, be an angel,' she went on imploringly. 'I'll really be in good with him if I can get him out of this mess.'

To Fliss's astonishment, the other girl suddenly looked deadly serious. Maybe it was true what Deb had more than once hinted about Lizzie's feelings for her boss.

'Well. . .' She hesitated, torn between her nervousness and her good nature. 'As soon as you've done the gram you get away, don't you?'

'Of course—no problem. Oh, thanks, pet.' Lizzie hugged her ecstatically. 'And you can borrow my black velvet cloak that you like so much,' she said over her shoulder, rushing back to the phone, and Fliss, feeling slightly sick, heard her say, 'Al? It's OK. . .'

An hour later, feeling even sicker, she stood in her tiny box-room bedroom as Lizzie, transformed into a nurse whose crotch-high skirt and low-cut top could never have graced even the most easygoing of hospital wards, gave the last few tweaks to her costume.

Finally, she stood back, surveying Fliss with satisfaction. 'You look great.' She propelled her over to the narrow mirror. 'Look.'

Fliss looked, her eyes dilated and she stepped back. Instinctively her hands came up, covering the luscious curves which, in the skimpy black lace basque, were all too obvious. Lizzie was only a couple of inches shorter than she was, and only a few pounds lighter, but oh, the difference.

'I *can't*!' she exclaimed.

'Of course you can.' The other girl shook her, almost angrily. 'What's the matter with you, for heaven's sake? Are you scared of your own body, or what? You are beautiful. No,' as Fliss half turned away. 'Look.'

And she was forced to stand, staring at the stranger reflected in the mirror, her eyes travelling slowly up the slim, endless legs encased in black fish-net stockings and suspenders, across the bare expanse of pale, silky thighs, the high-cut basque with its criss-cross opening which merely highlighted the voluptuousness of her body, then her bare shoulders and arms.

The girls had stood over her while she'd washed every bit of gel out of her hair and now it hung to her shoulders in a corn-gold cloud, framing her oval face, which Lizzie had skilfully made up to enhance its delicate beauty. A pair of wide sapphire eyes gazed back at her, stunned, and she fumbled for the sunglasses which were her habitual defence from the world, but they were snatched off her.

'Certainly not. You can have them back tomorrow. Now——' she tied a black velvet ribbon round Fliss's neck '—put my shoes on.' And, as she climbed obediently into the black stilettos, Lizzie, with a final tweak, stood back, grinning at her. 'Sweetie, you'll slay them.'

Outside, a car hooted and she lifted the curtain. 'That's your minicab.'

'But where am I going?'

'Don't worry. The driver'll know.'

'And whose party is it?'

'He's called Laslo—it's his birthday. He's a theatrical agent, so you never know,' she slanted a smile at her, 'play your cards right and this could be your lucky break.' Picking up the lovely black velvet cloak which lay on the bed, she flung it round Fliss's shoulders, then lightly pecked her cheek. 'Thanks. I shan't forget this.'

And Fliss, feeling distinctly unlike Cinderella going off to the ball, swept down to the entrance hall, the cloak making a little hissing noise from stair to stair. . .

The cab pulled up outside an apartment block off Bond Street and the driver consulted a scrap of paper.

'Flat 304. I'll wait.' As Fliss climbed slowly out he turned and something in her face seemed to penetrate his air of world-weary cynicism. 'Want me to come up with you, love?'

'No—no, I'll be all right, thanks.'

Inside, the caretaker lowered his evening paper just long enough to direct her to the lift, without the least flicker of interest, as though mysterious young women wrapped in black velvet cloaks were an every-evening occurrence.

No need, anyway, to ask where the party was. As soon as the lift opened, the throb of music hit her from the half-open door at the end of the plushly carpeted corridor. What had been clammy-palmed nervousness was changing rapidly into raging panic but she forced herself to walk towards the door. As she reached it, a man appeared from the dimness beyond, clutching a champagne bottle in one hand.

'You the kissogram girl?'

'Yes.' She had to shout to make herself heard above the din.

'Right. Let's go.'

Catching her icy hand in his hot one, he towed her through the hall and into the room beyond. Here, the noise level was so loud that it hit her like a physical blow, and strobe lights flickered through a haze of cigarette smoke. The crowd was thickest around an overweight, middle-aged man, who was flourishing an enormous cigar, and Fliss's guide dragged her through the melée towards him.

'Happy birthday, Laslo,' he yelled; then, as Fliss faltered, he gave her a shove so that she stumbled forward.

Fixing an empty smile to her mouth, she advanced on the man and then, just as Lizzie had schooled her to do, released the tie of her cloak, letting it fall to the ground. Shutting her ears to the chorus of shouts and whistles, she dodged the cigar and flung her arms round her quarry, planting a kiss on his cheek, well away from the fleshy lips.

As she drew back, she smiled warmly and said, 'Happy birthday, Laslo,' which was greeted with another raucous cheer and loud applause.

Well, at least her little performance seemed to have gone down well. Laslo whatever his name was grinning broadly as another man clapped him on the back. All she had to do was make a discreet exit, pick up her cab, and she'd be home in less than half an hour.

But, as she snatched up her cloak and went to back off through the throng, two men seized her by the arms. Before she could even begin to struggle, they had swung her round and dumped her on her feet on the long polished table which ran down one side of the room.

'Dance! Dance for Laslo!' they shouted and others joined in the call, clapping in a kind of disjointed rhythm.

She was surrounded by the mass of bodies pressing in on her. Humour them, she'd have to, just a while longer, and then they'd let her go. Fixing that empty smile in place again, she dropped her cloak on the table and began to pirouette up and down its length, her high heels slipping slightly on the gleaming surface. As the clapping rose to a crescendo, she came to a halt in front of Laslo, her arms outstretched, head and throat back, and one leg out in front of her.

For a moment she held the pose, then dropped her arms to her side and went to scramble down. But the crowd was up to the very edge of the table now, flushed faces turned towards her, and as she tried to climb off someone pushed her back.

'Strip!' She half thought she'd imagined the shout, but then the rest took it up, chanting 'Strip! Strip!' and the clapping started once more.

'*No!*' But the cry was torn out of her throat in a strangled whisper. She tried to get down again, kicking her high-heeled shoes off in the process, but hands thrust her roughly back, while she felt others tugging at the lacy edge of her basque. She shrank back against the wall, her fingers splayed against it. Suppose she screamed for help? But the cab driver wouldn't hear her, and, in an impersonal block of flats like this, who would come? Certainly not that caretaker three floors below.

Suddenly, through the clamour, she realised that the taped music had changed. Someone had put on the slow, languorous beat of 'The Stripper'. At the same moment the lights flickered, then a single red spotlight illuminated her, giving a metallic sheen to her costume and bathing her satiny skin in a dusky, sensuous glow.

At her feet the upturned faces, gleaming with sweat, had taken on a faint red tinge, as though from some nightmare, and Fliss, dizzy with terror, stood transfixed, so that if a way had opened through them she could not have moved.

'Strip! Strip!' The chanting began again, its insistent beat almost menacing now. With a sick helplessness she looked around her. There was no escape.

A hush had fallen on the crowd but the insidious beat of the music in her brain, the light streaming down on her, were dazing her so that she was beyond all coherent thought.

She paused, her eyes raking the mob at her feet in a mute appeal for mercy, but there was none. Then the door opened, an oblong of yellow light from the hall beyond fell into the hushed room, and a black outline stood framed in it. The figure paused, taking in the scene, then in half a dozen swift strides crossed the room.

Vaguely, she saw Laslo turn, heard him say, 'Hi, so you made it. You're just in time.' Then he was brushed out of the way as though he were a crawling insect and the man was reaching for her. As she stared down into his face, just for a moment, time jolted off its track, the years rolled away and she was back at Sombra, the night wind sighing in the branches, the night sky a blue-black velvet bowl above them.

And then, half fainting, she came off the table into the arms of Brand Carradine.

CHAPTER THREE

STILL barely conscious, Fliss felt Brand Carradine scoop up her cloak from the table and roughly wrap it round her.

'Hey. . .! What the hell. . .? Get back up there. . .!' The shouts bounced off her brain as he put his arm round her shoulders and began forcing his way through the tightly packed throng.

'Hold on, Brand.' Laslo's flushed face loomed in front of her. 'She's not leaving yet.'

Fliss felt the arm around her tense.

'Out of my way, damn you, Laslo.' Brand spoke very quietly between his teeth, but at the ice-cold anger in his voice the other man drew back and, his face set, he continued to cut a swathe through the gaping crowd to the door.

He steered her out through the entrance hall and along the corridor towards the lift.

'Here—put these on.'

He was holding her shoes out to her and, without a word, she took them. As she bent down, she glanced back over her shoulder and saw Laslo in the doorway, watching them. He looked rather pathetic. No— deflated, that was the word, and for a moment she almost felt sorry for him, so that she threw him a weak, half-apologetic smile, which he did not return.

Brand jabbed a vicious finger at the lift button and,

as the doors opened, pushed her inside. Overwrought as she was, she could feel the tears not far below the surface, and all at once she yearned to lay her head against that beautiful evening jacket, that pristine white shirt.

But then, seeing the hard, rigid lines of his face, instead she shrank into the corner, as far away from him as she could get, and wrapping the cloak even more closely around her began to do up the tie. But she could not control the trembling in her fingers and it kept slipping through them. She felt him watching her until finally, with an impatient exclamation, he pushed her hands out of the way and tied the bow, almost cutting into her throat.

As he pressed the ground-floor button, Fliss pulled up the hood and stood with her head averted.

'What's the matter?' His voice was harsh.

'Oh, nothing.' She still could not look at him. 'I-I was just thinking, I suppose we've spoilt his birthday.'

'Laslo?' He gave a short laugh in which humour was wholly lacking. 'Don't waste any sympathy on that bastard. Anyway, what the hell were you doing, a kid like you, in that place?'

The relief at being rescued, when all rescue had seemed impossible, was rapidly giving way to anger and shame. Of all the men in the world to witness her humiliation. . .

'Oh,' she muttered, 'it's a long story.'

'When I promised your grandfather I'd look you up when I was next in town——'

'Grampy?' she broke in eagerly. 'You've seen him? When?'

'Last week.'

'How is he?'

'All right. But then, Felicia, he doesn't know about what you're up to, does he?'

His words cut deep into her, so that she could almost hear her grandfather's voice when he'd learnt of some innocent schoolgirl prank—Oh, my dear child, the scrapes you get yourself into. As she bit her lip, the lift doors opened and, taking hold of her wrist, Brand pulled her out on to the pavement. The minicab was parked a little way up the street and as the driver spotted them he started the engine and cruised towards them.

'That's my cab,' she said. 'Goodnight, Mr Carradine, and thank you.' For the first time that evening she managed to look up full at him, meeting those chilly grey eyes. 'I really am grateful.'

But as the cab drew up Brand made no move to release her. He bent his head and said through the open window, 'You needn't wait. The lady's coming with me.'

As Fliss went rigid the driver glanced from one of the other; then she saw his lip curl slightly. 'If you say so, squire.'

Cringing with embarrassment, she stammered, 'It-it's all right. I know—I mean, we're old friends.'

The cabbie shrugged in patent disbelief but then put in the clutch and roared away.

Fliss rounded on Carradine furiously. 'Thanks very

much. You realise he thinks I've just picked you up
for the night l-like a——'

'Well, what do you expect?' His eyes raked contemptuously down and to her horror she realised that
in her agitation the cloak had swung open slightly, to
reveal the low-cut basque.

She clutched it to her as, putting his hand firmly
under her elbow, he steered her along the pavement
to where a bright red Lotus coupé was parked under
a street light. He unlocked the passenger door. 'In.'

'Suppose I don't?'

'Suppose you think about what's good for you.' He
spoke in the same very quiet voice he had used on
Laslo, and she scrambled in. Another time, she
promised herself, she'd stand up to this arrogant,
overbearing bully—but not tonight. He opened his
door, slid in beside her and they drew away from the
kerb.

'Camden, isn't it? Cobham Drive.'

Oh, Grampy. 'You obviously know, so why ask
me?' All remnants of that spurt of gratitude had
disappeared beneath her resentment and shame, and
she spent the rest of the journey staring straight
ahead through the windscreen in silence.

He pulled up outside her flat. 'This it?'

'Of course.'

Out of the corner of her eye, she saw him turn his
head sharply to look at her. 'Stop sulking. I don't like
sulky women.'

'Well, in that case, it's just as well we shan't be
setting eyes on each other after tonight, isn't it?
Goodnight.'

She got out, closed the door fairly quietly and headed up the steps, but, as she dug out the front-door key from her cloak pocket, a hand reached over her shoulder and took it from her. So he was determined to play it out to the very door of her flat, was he? Lifting the hem of her cloak lightly in both hands, she swept in and up the stairs.

From underneath the door, a chink of light showed. Lizzie back first. Or maybe Deb's stockbroker date hadn't worked out. But then, when she opened the door, her heart missed a beat. Sitting with his feet up on the low coffee-table, a whisky glass by his side, was Al. She turned and went to close the door in Brand's face, but he was right behind her and put up a hand to force it back.

'H-hello, Al.'

'Fliss, darling—you're back. Lizzie left the key out for me. How did it go?'

Clutching her cloak to her, she shifted uncomfortably. 'Oh—all right.'

She sneaked a sideways glance at the man standing beside her and saw that, eyes narrowed, he was taking in every last detail of the fair-haired young man in the pale grey, fashionably cut suit who was lounging on the sofa—and not much caring for what he was seeing. Al, too, was eyeing the newcomer warily.

'Er—this is Alan Rogers,' she said hastily. 'He runs the kissogram company.'

'Really? I'd never have guessed.' Brand's drawl stopped a hair's breadth from the edge of insolence, and as she saw the younger man flush Fliss rushed on.

'Al—meet Brandon Carradine. An old friend—from Jamaica,' she added, so that there could be no doubt.

'Brandon—did you say Brandon Carradine?' She was astonished to see Al gaping up at her. He set down his drink, spilling some of the contents, his eyes going from one to the other. '*The* Brand Carradine?'

'Are there any others?' Brand asked coolly.

What were they on about, for heaven's sake? It was Fliss's turn to stare at them both in bewilderment.

'Good grief.' Al was still shaking his head. 'Well, I'll be—I'm proud to meet you, Brand.'

He stood up, stretching out his hand, but Brand, not seeming to see it, merely nodded briefly, and after an uncomfortable pause Al dropped it to his side.

'What'll you have to drink?' A sideways glance at Fliss. 'I'm sure Lizzie won't mind sharing her best Scotch with Brand Carradine.'

'No, thanks.'

Al shrugged. 'Up to you. But I didn't know you were still on the showbiz scene, Brand. I thought you'd made your pile and got the hell out of it—but if you're looking for new investments I've got some ideas I'm sure you'd be interested in.'

'I don't think so.'

Fliss winced inwardly at the curt put-down but Al was not so easily deflected. 'I'm moving into the music promotion business, building a nice little stable of groups. One of them's bound to hit the big time—

and if you care to come in with me before lift off——'

'I've told you—no.' That chipped-ice tone again, which halted even Al's sales pitch in its tracks.

'Oh, well, don't say I didn't give you the chance. Anyway, sweetheart,' he turned to Fliss, 'I was passing the door, so I thought I'd just look in and say thanks for helping out tonight.'

For the first time, it occurred to her that maybe Al had just 'looked in', knowing that she would be back some time before Lizzie finished her two stints. She smiled ironically to herself. Perhaps, for the second time this evening, she ought actually to be grateful to have Brand by her side.

'I've got your money—cash, of course.' From his inside pocket he drew out a fat wallet, and as she watched, every fibre of her squirming with humiliated awareness of the other man's sardonic eyes on her, he counted out four crisp ten-pound notes into her hand.

'And remember, darling, any time you want to make a bit of the ready, just give me a bell.'

'She won't be doing that, Rogers.' All pretence at civility had gone from Brand's tone. 'That was the last kissogram—or anything else—that she does for you.'

How dare he? She'd vowed that very thing a hundred times to herself already tonight, but who was he to say what she did or didn't do?

'Oh? And why's that?' Al demanded belligerently.

'Mainly because I say so——'

'Now, look here——' Bristling with anger, Fliss crushed the notes as her hands made fists.

'—but also because she is having nothing more to do with any sleazy outfit that you run.'

'What the hell do you mean—sleazy outfit? Let me tell you——'

'You realise she could have landed herself in a whole lot of trouble tonight?' He was talking about her almost as though she weren't there. 'When I arrived, they'd just reached the striptease stage.'

'Oh, no.' Al laughed. 'Don't tell me Laslo was up to his tricks again. Karen had the same trouble last year—but it's all a bit of harmless fun, Fliss.'

Besides her, she heard the hissed intake of fury. 'Harmless fun—with *Laslo*? You mean that, knowing that evil toad's reputation with young girls, you sent this *child*——' Child? Who was he calling child? '—there, to face him on her own?'

'Well, she was hardly on her own. And anyway, Carradine, don't you tell me my business. Just because you struck lucky——'

Brand picked up the fawn lightweight mac which lay across one of the chairs and slung it at him. 'Out.'

'Now, just you wait a minute.' Al's face flushed a dark red.

'Unless you want me to throw you out.'

Al took an instant measure of their respective builds and shrugged. 'Don't worry, I'm going anyway.' With an attempt at casualness, he drained his glass. 'Bye, Fliss.'

He moved as though to kiss her but then, obviously catching Brand's steely eye, thought better of it. 'Well—see you around. Cheers, Carradine. Now I've met you, I can see what people mean about you.'

Before the outside door had quite closed, Fliss swung round, her temper boiling over. 'How dare you? This is my flat, and if there's any throwing out to be done I'll do it—and I'll damn well make a start with you. Get out.'

His dark brows levelled in a faint frown of displeasure, but his only response was to lower himself into one of the armchairs. The deliberate action inflamed her still further.

'And how dare you tell Al that that was my last job for him? I'll work as a 'gram girl every night of the week if I choose to.'

'Well, you were certainly enjoying yourself tonight, I'll give you that.' He regarded her contemptuously. 'You seemed to be having nearly as much fun as your audience, keeping them on tenterhooks like that.'

'Oh.' The injustice of his words caught her by the throat. And yet—perhaps when he'd arrived her agonised reluctance just might have looked like a tantalising pretence. But who was he—of all men—to set himself up as judge and jury of her behaviour? 'F-for your information, that was my very first kissogram tonight. And I only did it as a favour for my flat-mate.'

'Really?'

His look of patent disbelief enraged her even more, so she went on defiantly, 'I know things got out of hand, but with a bit more experience I'll be able to handle a situation like that—and without any help from you.'

'Hmm. Well, I'm afraid that, Felicia, is something which will have to stay unproven.'

'Please, *Mr* Carradine,' she said through her teeth, 'not Felicia. Only my grandfather calls me that.'

'Very well—Fliss. And perhaps you'll be good enough to drop the Mr Carradine bit. Call me Brand. Everyone does—including your grandfather.'

But she didn't want to call him by his first name. 'Mr Carradine': it was like a security fence, erected to keep him at arm's length, and as long as he was safely at a distance maybe she wouldn't have to remember. . . She became aware of his grey eyes watching her.

'Anyway, you haven't really told me how Grampy was when you saw him.'

'As I said—he's all right.' He hesitated fractionally. 'He seemed quite relieved, though, when I promised him that I'd keep an eye on you.'

'*What?*' Appalled, she could only stare at him, her eyes dilating.

'He worries about you, you know—a young girl, on her own in London. So, as I was coming over here, I said I'd be happy to——'

'Spy on me,' she flared. 'Check up on my morals, and then report back, I suppose. My God,' she gave a bitter laugh, 'who the hell do you think you are, daring to sit in moral judgement on me?'

'And just what do you mean by that?'

His eyes, narrowed like a cat's, seemed to bore right into her and she teetered on the brink of revelation. But he must never know who she was, never have the slightest inkling that she was the girl by the pool on that moonlit night at Sombra. The shame and humiliation would be too much to bear.

'Well——' she improvised '—you were at that party tonight. You're a friend of Laslo's.'

'Not a friend, exactly. But in my business you can't choose all your acquaintances.'

'Just what is your——?'

A key turned in the lock and the next moment Deb, clutching on to a smartly dressed but vacuous-looking young man, burst in.

'Hi, Fliss.'

As they both collapsed on to the sofa Fliss's heart sank. Deb's hair was dishevelled, and they were both obviously the worse for drink. She did not dare look in Brand's direction.

'Hello, Deb.'

'Well, aren't you going to introduce us?'

Fliss winced as the older girl's blue eyes appraised Brand, taking in every detail of him. 'He's an old friend—from the West Indies.'

'Really? Well, you'll have lots to talk about, then.' Getting to her feet, she pulled her companion up with her, then ran one fingertip lazily down his tie, murmuring something in his ear. 'Excuse us,' she said, and together they disappeared through Deb's bedroom door.

Fliss groaned inwardly, and a wild desire to laugh, and keep on laughing, took hold of her. All that was needed was for Lizzie, still in her Sexy Little Nurse outfit, to arrive home and her evening would be complete.

'Right.' Brand had leapt to his feet, his face grim. 'Get yourself changed and pack your things.'

'What?' She gaped at him, all the hysterical laughter frozen. 'What do you mean?'

'What I say. You aren't staying in this place another night.'

'I'm not hearing you right.' She shook her head. 'This is my home. Where on earth do you expect me to go?'

'Just pack and you'll find out.'

Deliberately, she sat down and carefully folded her arms across her chest. 'Sorry, but I'm not going anywhere—with anybody. And least of all with you.'

'Why have you brought me here?' Fliss demanded, looking suspiciously around the spacious, beautifully furnished sitting-room of the penthouse apartment.

'This is my flat, of course—my base when I'm in London.'

'Your——?' It was almost a squeak. 'Well, I'm not staying here.'

'I'm afraid you are—temporarily, at least.' As if to reinforce his words, Brand set down her case. He gave her a level look but then, as she backed up against the wall, trying vainly to cover her sudden nervousness with a defiant glare, his lips twisted. 'Oh, don't worry, my dear Fliss. I promise you, you're safer with me than with any other man in England.'

'Am I?' The hasty words leapt out as, too late, she tried to bite them back. 'I-I mean, you all but kidnap me. . .' she shot him a resentful glare; one wrist was still tingling from when she had been practically frogmarched down to Brand's car, protesting violently every inch of the way '. . .and bring me here. Well, I-I'll not stand for it.'

She swallowed, choking at the total unreasonableness of the man. He had barely given her time to scramble her possessions together, shed the hated basque, and climb into old pale blue jeans and a navy fisherman's sweater.

'I think you will,' he said curtly, 'if only because, if you try to leave, well——' He broke off with a meaningful glance.

'You'll tell Grampy I'm spending my time performing sleazy stripteases, I suppose.'

'Something like that, yes.'

Her shoulders sagged. He was treating her as though she were a recalcitrant child of five, she thought bitterly. But there was an undercurrent in his voice which made her shrink from rousing the sleeping tiger of his anger and she just muttered, 'You can't keep me here forever, you know.'

'Perhaps not—but for the time being there's no problem, so sit down and make yourself at home.' Make herself at home—in this tiger's den? Even so, she dropped into the nearest white leather armchair.

He sat down opposite, regarding her thoughtfully. 'Have you got a job you should be going to in the morning?'

'Not really.' She hesitated; it was no business of his whatsoever. 'If you must know, I was intending to start another stint working in the kitchens of an Italian restaurant round the corner from my flat.'

He raised his eyebrows questioningly. 'Your grandfather told me you're an actress.'

'Well.' She pulled a face. 'That's what I want to be, but I haven't made it yet. I shall do, though—I know I shall,' she added defiantly.

'Hmm. You know, you've chosen a pretty tough profession to break into.'

She permitted herself a wry smile. 'You don't need to tell me that. In fact, I'm beginning to think——' She broke off abruptly.

'Yes?'

'Oh, nothing.' She'd been about to admit the truth—that just lately she'd been seriously facing up to the idea that maybe she really didn't have enough talent, that it would almost be a relief to give up all her hopes and ambitions. But instead she merely said, 'No doubt you'd agree with my drama tutor. He said,' she attempted a comical grimace, 'that I'm too wild and undisciplined to make a good actress.'

'Oh, Fliss,' he said softly, and as she stared at him, arrested by something in his tone, he smiled at her. It was the first time she had really seen him smile, his taut mouth easing to show his white, even teeth, the little lines around his grey eyes creasing up, and the effect was as though someone had without warning kicked her hard in the region of her midriff.

Unable to control the sudden turmoil inside her, she leapt up and went over to the long window. Standing with her back to him, she rested her head against her hand, gazing out. The penthouse overlooked the Thames, and lights reflected from its blue-black depths like a drowned sky, while a car's headlights briefly illuminated the bare, wintry trees on the far side of the water.

Over there, somewhere past that string of dull orange street-lights, was surely where she'd spent her childhood, until the traumatic events which had rent that childhood in two. Her mother had died and, far too quickly, her father had remarried.

Of course, the rift had been partly her fault, the twenty-year-old Fliss acknowledged with a new insight. Still grieving for the mother she had lost, she had viewed the intruder with implacable hostility; refusing to allow her or her father to come near her emotionally, Fliss had hugged her unhappiness to her like a favourite teddy-bear.

When her father had announced that they were emigrating to New Zealand, where his brother was already farming, Fliss had dug her heels in defiantly and it had seemed the best solution all round when her grandfather had gladly offered her a home in Jamaica. But even so she'd never really got over the feeling of not being wanted, of being abandoned. . .

'Of course, you used to live over that way, didn't you?' Brand's voice, very casual, made her start.

'How do you know?' Without turning, she met his eyes reflected in the window.

'Oh, your grandfather was telling me.'

Was there anything about her that he and Grampy had not discussed? 'And he told you the rest, I suppose?'

'Some of it, Fliss.'

She turned and saw a soft, almost tender expression on his face which rasped on her raw nerves. 'Oh, save your sympathy. You'll be telling me next that I'm a poor motherless child who needs taking care of.'

'Perhaps.' He smiled faintly at the vehemence of her tone.

'Well, I don't want anyone's pity. And most of all I don't want it from *you*.'

The lines of his face snapped back into their customary hardness. 'I'll show you to your room.'

Picking up her case, he preceded her down the deeply carpeted passage and into what was clearly a seldom-used guest room. 'Your bathroom's through there.' He gestured briefly towards the far door. 'I'll be back in a few minutes.'

When he had gone, she plumped down on to the bed. She was dreaming—she had to be; she must have gone straight to bed after the disaster of that kissogram, and now she was in the middle of a terrible nightmare, in which Brand Carradine had come back into her life to disrupt it exactly as he'd disrupted it four years before.

But the cream carpet under her feet felt solid enough, the chocolate-brown counterpane, as she drew her fingers across it, was real enough. And there, in the dressing-table mirror, was her reflection—pale, distraught face and shadowed eyes. . .

When Brand came back, she was still sitting there, her fingers plucking irresolutely at the zip of her case. He had changed into a casual grey cord suit and black ribbed polo sweater, and had clearly taken time to shower, for a faint aroma of soap and spicy aftershave hung in the air about him, teasing her nostrils. He was carrying a slim attaché case, which he placed on the bare dressing-table, and stood looking down at her.

'I have to go out.'

'*Out?* But it's well after eleven.'

'Yes, well—some of the people I do business with keep late hours. I'd planned to see someone at Laslo's tonight, but. . .'

As he broke off with a slight shrug, curiosity overcame her determination not to show the slightest interest in him. 'Just what is your business?'

'Well, as your friend Al suggested, I'm on the fringes of show business. I suppose you could call me a kind of showbiz venture capitalist.'

When she looked at him blankly, he went on, 'Mainly, I finance shows—musicals, in particular— before they go into production, and if they're a success I get a slice of the profits. It's a risky game, but I've managed to pick one or two winners the last few years that have been big on Broadway as well as the West End.'

'So that's what Al meant—about you being lucky, I mean.'

'I wouldn't call it luck. I started with nothing, made my first few hundred selling tapes and records in a street market when I was still at school, and went on from there. And I don't call it lucky to have spotted the potential in writers before anyone else and had the courage to back them when nobody else would touch their shows.' He picked up his case, then paused. 'If you're hungry, there's plenty of food in the fridge.'

'No, thank you. I won't bother.' She was looking

down, her blonde hair masking her face as she traced the carpet pattern with the toe of her shoe.

'Well, if you change your mind,' he went on evenly, 'help yourself. I may be late, so don't wait up. Oh, and Fliss,' he paused in the doorway, 'I hope you haven't any ideas about leaving. Jackson, the hall porter, is under instructions not to let you past him— and I've also told him to hold any outgoing phone calls from here until I get back. Goodnight.'

'Oh, you—get lost!' she yelled at the closing door then, snatching up one of the crisp linen pillows, she hurled it across the room.

Just who does he think he is? No, don't tell me, she thought despairingly. Brand Carradine. Are there any others? he'd said in that voice, smooth as silk, arrogant as a peacock. And everyone reacted the way they were supposed to—backing off slightly, clearing a space round him. At Laslo's, no one had made any real effort to stop him leaving with her. As for Al, a tough young East-Ender—Brand hadn't raised his voice, yet he had made an undignified exit; she'd heard his footsteps retreating rapidly down the stairs. And she herself had been intimidated into coming here with him, when all her instincts had fought against it. Presumably that was how he always operated: a touch of good old-fashioned terror, to cow business rivals, aggressive twenty-year-old girls— anybody who got in his way—into gibbering submission.

Well, was she going to bow her neck meekly before this tyrant? No, of course not. She really had nothing to fear from him, whether she remained in this flat or not. And yet. . . Certainly, he'd behaved with ultra-correctness since meeting up with her again—apart, that was, from kidnapping her.

The few times they'd come close enough to make physical contact—when he'd taken her case from her in her flat, when he'd tied the bow of her cloak in the lift at Laslo's—she'd had the distinct impression that he had made sure that his fingers did not brush against her skin, almost as though he couldn't bear to touch her. And yet he was the man who, four years ago by that pool at Sombra, had taken her with such lethal ease. . .

Snatching up her case, she raced along the passage, silently opened the front door of the penthouse, and listened. All was quiet apart from the soft beat of music from one of the apartments below. Closing the door behind her, she paused a moment longer to slip on her beige trench coat, then tiptoed along to the stairway, not daring to risk the lift.

But suppose this Mr Jackson was on patrol in the entrance lobby? No—the fire escape at the far end of the corridor was her best bet. The bar was difficult to budge, but at last it lifted. She stepped on to the metal platform outside and came face to face with Brand, just as he ran lightly up the last few steps.

He stood for a moment, taking in her coat and case, then shook his head in exasperation. 'Going somewhere?'

'Yes, home,' she said through her teeth and took a firmer grip on her case, then had to watch in helpless silence as he peeled her fingers away one by one.

But back in his sitting-room she rounded on him.

'I suppose all that charade about you going out was just a trap for me?'

'Not at all. But fortunately I remembered some papers I need.'

He locked the front door then, as Fliss stood stormy-eyed, he slipped the key into his jacket pocket.

'Aren't you going, then?'

He regarded her, his lips pursed, until she grew nervous under his speculative gaze. All he said, though, was, 'You know, you are becoming rather a pain in the neck——'

'I'm so glad.'

'—so I think, on balance, it'll be better if I do business by phone on this occasion.'

As he dropped down into one of the leather chairs, drawing the phone towards him, she went across and stood glowering down at him.

'I shan't be long. Sit down.' He waved a casual hand towards another chair.

'No, I'm going to bed.'

'That's right. Get a good night's sleep.' He scarcely glanced at her. 'I'm flying back to Jamaica tomorrow, and you're coming with me.'

And as she gaped at him, her eyes darkening with horrified stupefaction, he turned away. 'Richard. Glad I've caught you. It's Brand—sorry I missed you earlier. About that show you're trying to get lined up. . .'

CHAPTER FOUR

'MORNING, Mr Carradine. Nice to see you back, sir.' The young woman in the airport immigration section smiled broadly then waved them and their cases through with the most cursory of glances.

Huh. The full VIP treatment. Fliss aimed a hostile glare at Brand's shoulder-blades as she followed him through the arrivals lounge. All the times she'd landed here, she'd never had this invisible red carpet put down for her. . . A porter looking out for their luggage as it came through on the carousel. . .ushered through Customs. . .and now a smartly dressed young man, who had been lounging against the counter chatting to a check-in girl, was hurriedly straightening up and coming over to them.

'Morning, Mr Carradine. It's the black Chevy in the parking lot.'

As he handed Brand the keys, his eyes strayed in her direction then widened in recognition. 'Why, hi there, Fliss!'

She stared at him, then a warm smile broke through on her tense face. 'Scott! How lovely to see you. How are you?'

'Oh, fine.' His brown eyes swiftly took in every detail of her. 'Hey, you're looking great, Fliss.'

'Thank you.' She flushed with pleasure and even

managed a teasing grin. 'You're not looking so bad yourself. And how's everybody?'

But before Scott could reply Brand had said curtly, 'Excuse us,' his hand closed over her elbow and he was leading her firmly away.

Over her shoulder she called defiantly to Scott, who was watching them with a faintly speculative gaze, 'We must get together some time while I'm here.'

Once outside, she stopped dead. 'Let me go—and stop treating me as if I'm some kind of criminal, will you?'

Shaking her arm free, she scowled up at him, but his only response was an amused smile. While she felt like a cat dancing around on red-hot bricks, he was completely, infuriatingly relaxed. But of course he'd won, hadn't he? Won that battle of wills which had raged through his penthouse half the previous night and had only ended with the white flag of surrender—temporarily, she'd promised herself—as she'd gone up the steps of the first jumbo out of Heathrow this morning.

Now she got into the passenger seat of the sleek black car in silence and stared ahead as the porter loaded their cases into the boot. Brand reversed, then drove down the avenue, lined at this time of year with sprawling mauve and pink bougainvillaea, then turned out on to the main road which led to town.

How beautiful it all was. In spite of her mood, a little smile played around her mouth. She'd been out here at Christmas, and yet she'd forgotten already— as surely everyone did—just how dazzling the heat was, how brilliant the shimmer of the sky, the colours, the scents drifting in through the open windows, and to the left, through a gap in the trees, the sea. . . And gradually, imperceptibly, her anger at being manipulated—and manhandled—by the arrogant swine beside her, the irritation with herself at being so spineless, and even her trepidation over exactly what he intended telling her grandfather—it all evaporated in the intense, blazing joy of being back home.

Almost before Brand had pulled up at the house, she was out and running up the steps.

'Grampy!'

The green mesh door opened and Maybelle came out, her face drawn, her eyes swollen.

'Oh, my honey——' she began, and burst into loud, sobbing tears.

'What is it?' Terror was clutching Fliss by the throat so that she could hardly get the words out. 'He's ill. I must go to him.'

But as she went to push blindly past the stout figure, another pair of hands captured her.

'Let me go, damn you!' She tore herself free from Brand's grasp but then, as she caught the look which passed between him and the housekeeper, she flung her hands up to her ears.

'No!' she cried, and again, 'No, no, no!' as though, by denying it, she would make the unbearable not true, and then, as her knees buckled, a vortex of dizziness caught her and whirled her away into blackness. . .

* * *

She opened her eyes and half raised her head but then, as she felt the bed beneath her, saw the light filtering in through the almost-closed louvres, she let it fall back on to the pillow.

There was a faint movement, then a voice said softly, 'Felicia—how are you, my dear girl?'

John Barrett, the doctor whom she had known since she was a child, was sitting on a cane chair beside her bed, and as she stared up at him he took her hand, repeating, 'How are you?'

'All right,' she said in a dreary little voice.

He squeezed her hand then laid it on the cotton counterpane. 'Shall I ask Maybelle to sit with you? Or perhaps you'd rather Mrs Bailey came. She rang up a little while ago and will come if you want her.'

They were all being so kind. Tears filled her eyes and she turned her head away, biting her lip.

'There's no need to send for anyone.'

Another voice had spoken and looking round she saw, through the blur of her tears, Brand. He had been leaning against the window-frame, his arms folded; now, he straightened up and came across to the bed, though he did not look at her.

'She won't be on her own,' he said firmly. 'I shall be here with her.'

'Er—well, in that case——' The doctor looked from one to the other then stood up, gazing down at her. 'Now be a sensible girl and try and get some sleep. I'll call in again tomorrow.'

He patted her arm then turned away, but as she closed her eyes she heard him say in an undertone, 'I'll leave these with you.' There was a faint rattle.

'Try and persuade her to have two—they'll help her sleep.'

Still with her eyes closed, she heard the soft creak as Brand settled himself in the chair, then he said very gently, 'Fliss.'

The tenderness in his voice caught her, getting past all her defences. 'Mmm?' she said in a choked whisper, then pressed her knuckles to her mouth as from very deep inside her a huge sob rose and burst out.

'Oh—I'm s-sorry,' she wept, struggling to fight down her anguish, then next moment she felt Brand move on to the bed and raise her into his arms, cradling her head against his chest. 'No. I don't want to cry.'

She was holding herself stiffly, fighting for control, but he said urgently, 'No, Fliss—cry. Let it all out,' and then clasped her tightly as a tumult of pain and grief burst over her head.

At last the tears dried and she was still, apart from an occasional shuddering spasm. He held her away from him and looked down at her, his face sombre. 'Better?'

She gave a little nod then caught sight of his wet, crumpled shirt-front. 'Oh, I've messed up your shirt.' But he only shook his head, then took a folded handkerchief from his trouser pocket and wiped her sore eyes before laying her back down on the pillow.

'You should try and sleep now. The doctor——'

'No!' she said vehemently. 'I want to—Brand, tell me please,' her voice trembled dangerously, 'how did it happen?'

He hesitated, then said, 'Yesterday morning, he

took his old boat out to the reef and did a dive. He brought up some coral and spent the afternoon doing a painting of it. And then this morning, when Maybelle went to his room, she found him; he'd died peacefully in his sleep. Fliss,' he took her hand in both of his, 'he didn't suffer, not at all—you must hang on to that,' as her eyes filled with tears again, 'and, after a morning out on the reef, and an afternoon painting, well, he went just as he would have wished, if he could have chosen.'

'But——' in her agitation she was plucking at the buttons on his shirt '—but you told me he was worried about me.'

He gave her just the faintest of smiles. 'Because you are a naughty, wilful, undisciplined young woman, you mean?' But then, when he saw her expression, he went on quickly, 'No, my sweet. You must never, ever think that you had anything to do with his death.'

He paused momentarily again. 'He's had a heart condition for some time. Dr Barrett had warned him that he really should give up diving—but can you imagine anyone telling J. G. Sinclair that?' His lips flickered slightly. 'And he wouldn't allow anyone to tell you. He loved you so much, you know—he talked about you all the time. The last time I saw him, he told me you were the light of his life, and I know that you made him very happy.'

'Even if I am a naughty, wilful, undisciplined young woman.' Fliss managed a wan smile. 'Thank you for telling me, Brand.'

'You must sleep now. I'll get you one of Dr Barrett's pills.'

'No, please. I'll sleep without that. Although——' she looked up at him, her mouth drooping '—I don't want to be alone. Please stay with me.'

'Oh, Fliss. I. . .' He lifted his hand, and began to brush the tousled hair from her brow, but then all at once his fingers stilled and he withdrew them abruptly. 'Of course I'll stay with you. I told Barrett I would.' But the sudden formality in his tone chilled her. 'I'll get Maybelle to undress you.' And before she could protest that she could manage perfectly well, he had gone.

When he returned, she was lying on her back in her white cotton nightie, her hair combed around her face. Drowsy with sleep, she smiled up at him but he did not respond, only moved the chair back away from the bed and sat down.

She turned on her side towards him and held out her hand beseechingly. 'Please, Brand—hold me.'

For a moment, she thought he would resist her, but then at last he kicked off his shoes, lowered himself down on the counterpane and drew her very gently towards him. She settled her head in the crook of his shoulder, his unshaven chin rasping softly against the fine hairs at her temple, then closed her eyes.

'Goodbye—and thank you for coming.'

Fliss waved off another group of funeral guests then, feeling the smile which had been so painfully tacked in place for the last two hours begin to slip, she turned back to the house.

Most people had already left—only a few were draining their drinks, prior to murmuring their final condolences and leaving. She wandered back into the big reception-room, so little used in her grandfather's time, now gleaming and polished by Maybelle and filled with flowers. Their scent was overpowering, transporting her back to the funeral service in the little parish church and the burial overlooking Grampy's beloved Caribbean, and hastily she moved over to the open doorway.

Jim and Sue Bailey, her grandfather's oldest friends on the island, were sitting out on the veranda. Brand was with them, and she stood in the shadows, pretending to watch all of them but seeing only him.

Until the funeral, she hadn't set eyes on him since the day of their arrival. When she'd woken, he was gone, leaving only a scrawled message that if she wanted anything at all she was to send for him. She'd stared down at that hurried message with a strange sense of being bereft, but even before she'd realised that Sue had arrived to take care of everything she'd known that she couldn't possibly send for him.

'Fliss, my dear.'

She turned back into the room to say more goodbyes, then stood, alone for the first time that day except for her reflection in the long mirror opposite. She was wearing a turquoise linen dress; not exactly conventional funeral-wear, but she'd chosen it deliberately for her grandfather had always liked her best in turquoise—the colour of the sea. But the pretty shade could not disguise the tautness of her mouth, the dark smudges under her eyes.

Perhaps, when they'd all gone, she'd go off down to the beach for a couple of hours, start picking up the threads of her life again. Straightening her shoulders, she went out to the veranda.

'Ah, there you are, Flissy.' Jim Bailey, so stiff and unlike his usual self in his dark suit, smiled kindly up at her. 'Everyone else gone?'

'Yes.'

She looked only at him, but with every particle of her body she was aware of the other man. She heard him get to his feet, turned slowly to him, and for a moment they regarded one another in silence. He too, she realised, looked as though he had not been sleeping well. Under his tan his face was pale, the hard planes of his face even sharper than usual.

'Goodbye, Fliss.' He took her hand, his eyes shadowed. 'If you need anything——'

'Thank you,' she said brusquely, 'but I shall be all right.'

'Oh, don't go just yet, Brand, if you don't mind.'

Jim set down his drink and stood up. Fliss, glancing from one to the other, saw Brand frown very slightly then give an almost imperceptible shrug. 'Of course.'

As though on cue, Sue was lifting her comfortable bulk out of the wicker chair. 'I'll go on, then.' She took Fliss in her arms. 'Now remember, honey, if you want me, just shout. And you're sure you won't come and stay with us at Prospect Hill—just for a few days, at least?'

Dear Sue—always searching for shorn lambs to

cherish. Fliss smiled into her comfortable bosom then, feeling her eyes fill with weak tears, drew back. 'Thank you, Sue, but I'm all right, honestly.'

The three of them stood, a rather awkward little group, until Sue drove off; then Jim cleared his throat. 'Well, Fliss, perhaps we could go indoors?' As she looked blankly at him, he added gently, 'The will, my pet.'

'Oh.' She had all but forgotten that Jim Bailey, as well as being Grampy's friend for years, was also his lawyer. 'Oh, yes—come in.'

As she led the way into the reception-room, she heard Brand say something in an undertone, then Jim's reply, 'Yes, Brand, I want you here.'

Maybelle had opened the louvres and they sat at the beautiful old table, made of island mahogany, the two men at either end, Fliss in the centre so that she need look only at Jim. She watched as he drew out from his inside pocket two sheets of foolscap paper, unfolded them in front of him, then got out his spectacles and put them on.

For a moment there was silence in the room, and all at once she felt something—a slight tension which was hardly more than a breath—begin to make itself felt, and when she glanced from under her lashes at Brand she saw that his long fingers were beating a soundless tattoo on the table, as though he too was aware of that tension. And yet, surely, Grampy had had very little to leave. . .

'First, for my loyal housekeeper of many years, Maybelle Dolores Wilmot. . .' Jim began, in his most lawyer-like tones.

Good. Fliss gave a tiny inner smile. She'd intended to give Maybelle as much as she could afford, but it was far better that Grampy had done it formally.

'. . .ten thousand dollars.'

Fliss somehow restrained her exclamation of dismay. Surely, Grampy's estate wasn't worth that in total? Somehow, though—she set her soft lips determinedly—she'd make up the rest, to ensure that his wishes were——'

'For Brandon Carradine, the original water-colour paintings from my book, which he so admired.'

So that was why Jim had wanted him here. Just for a moment, the memory flooded back of that day, over four years ago, when she'd seen him here, so engrossed in the paintings that—thankfully—he'd barely even noticed the pigtailed schoolgirl.

But then, looking full at him for the first time, she gave him a warm smile. 'I'm so pleased, Brand. He knew how much you liked them.'

'And to my beloved granddaughter, Felicia Emily Naughton, the house—that it may always be a refuge for her—and the residue of my estate.'

Those weak tears were threatening yet again. She stared down at the table as Brand asked, 'And how much will that be, Jim?'

Well, really. It was none of his business, none at all. She looked up, flushing with irritation, as Jim replied, 'Well, of course, I haven't got the exact figure to hand yet, but somewhere in the region of a quarter of a million.'

'What? That's impossible!'

'Jamaican dollars, I presume?'

She and Brand both spoke together, but Jim answered him. 'Yes.'

'But——' she began ineffectually.

'And as the dollar is linked to the US currency,' Brand went on, 'at the present exchange rate, that's worth approaching two hundred thousand pounds.'

'But there must be some mistake.' Fliss raised her voice. 'Grampy had hardly any money. Oh, I know he paid a lot for my education, but he——'

'Your grandfather didn't choose to lead a lavish lifestyle, true,' Jim interposed, 'but that was because he preferred to save it—for you, my dear.' Fliss stared at him, a hard knot forming in her chest. 'His book has never been out of print, and still sells pretty well, I believe. And he invested wisely on the stock market—oh, ten years ago, about the time you first came out here to live with him.'

'But—but I had no idea.'

'No.' Jim's face relaxed into a slight smile. 'I think James felt that, while he'd been so indulgent with you in so many ways, it was better for you to make your own way in the world, for a few years at least. But now that he's. . .'

His voice tailed off and Fliss said huskily, 'I see. Well—thank you, Jim. But now, if there's nothing further——'

'I haven't quite finished, Fliss.' He cleared his throat again. 'There is one other clause.'

'Another bequest, you mean?'

'Well—no,' he said awkwardly, shuffling the papers between his fingers.

That faint whisper of tension had crept insidiously back. 'Well—go on,' she urged.

'Your twenty-first birthday is in five months' time.'

'That's right. On August the twenty-second.' Her brow puckered. What on earth had that to do with anything? But then her frown cleared. 'Oh, of course, you still don't come of age out here until you're twenty-one, do you? So there's some legal thing to stop me inheriting till then, is that it?'

'Well—not exactly.' Jim still sounded highly uncomfortable. 'You must understand that your grandfather was very concerned about you, Fliss. He blamed himself for having, as he saw it, spoilt you so much.' She shot a swift glance at Brand, and caught the sardonic gleam in his eye. 'And so he was anxious, if anything should happen to him, that you should be taken care of—at least until you officially come of age. And so——'

'So?' she demanded impatiently.

'And so, until you are twenty-one, he has appointed Brandon Carradine to be your legal guardian.'

CHAPTER FIVE

'WHAT?'

They both spoke simultaneously again, then Fliss leapt to her feet, her chair tumbling to the floor behind her. Her eyes flew from Brand, who was looking at least as appalled as she felt, to Jim.

'It's not true!' she cried. 'It can't be true.'

'Well, now, Flissy.' He too was standing up, as though anxious to be off before the hurricane struck. 'I knew you wouldn't be best pleased about it, but he was adamant.'

'When did he insert that clause?'

'Oh—about a year ago. Soon after he came back to Jamaica and John Barrett began to be concerned about his health.'

'But why Brand Carradine, of all people?'

'Precisely—I couldn't have put it better myself,' Brand chipped in drily. 'Why me?'

'Well, I know James had a high regard for you——'

'But if I was to have a guardian at all, why didn't he choose you?' Fliss wailed. 'You were his oldest friend.'

Jim pulled a face. 'Yes, but James never made any secret of the fact that he thought that Sue and I spoilt Perry something rotten after her parents were killed.

And in any case, maybe he thought you'd do better with someone younger to—er—take care of you.'

'I'll not stand for it.' Fliss tossed back her mane of fair hair. 'It—it's treating me as if I'm a child.'

'Well, you know that's the way he always regarded you, pet,' Jim said pacifically. 'And it's only for a short while. After all, what's five months? Less than half a year.'

Half a year? She shuddered at the thought. Half a lifetime, more like, with that overbearing tyrant in charge of her. True, he'd been marvellous to her, helping her through the first dreadful shock when they'd arrived, but anyone with an ounce of feeling in them would have done as much, and now, given absolute *carte blanche* to treat her just as he wished, he'd no doubt immediately revert to his old arrogant, high-handed self.

In just one night in London—she writhed inwardly at the memory of that hopelessly unequal battle of wills in his flat—she'd had a sample of exactly how he could behave. And that was when Grampy had only asked him to 'keep an eye on her'. But now, with the full weight of the law behind him. . .

'Does the will set out the specific terms of this guardianship?' Brand asked, his voice clipped.

'Er—yes, it does. You exercise full control over Fliss's financial affairs——'

'What?' Fliss was all but speechless.

'—and,' Jim lowered his head to read from the document, 'you are to take full responsibility for her moral welfare.'

'Moral welfare?'

Before Fliss could prevent herself, her eyes flew to Brand and she saw his own eyes darken, his lips thin to a taut line. If Grampy had only known. . . The hysteria was bubbling up inside her, and hastily she turned back to Jim.

'So try and not make any trouble, chuck.' He gave her a look which was almost pleading.

'Why? What happens if I do?'

'Well, that will be up to Brand,' he said unhappily. He put his arm round her and kissed her cheek. 'But I know it won't come to that,' and, with an encouraging squeeze, he fled.

She waited until his steps had died away, then swung round on Brand, still sitting transfixed at the far end of the table.

'Did you know about this?' she demanded.

He gave a brief, wholly mirthless laugh. 'What do you think? Do you imagine for one minute that I would have agreed to such a crazy scheme?' He ran his fingers distractedly through his thick black hair. 'Oh, God—it's impossible.'

'In that case, let's forget it, shall we?' Picking up her chair, she sank down into it. 'Look, we can just pretend——'

'Don't be a little fool,' he said harshly. 'Your grandfather has landed—*entrusted* me with this, and I'll do my damnedest to carry out his wishes.'

'Yes, and won't you just enjoy it?' she snarled.

'No, I shan't, as a matter of fact.' But he did not say it angrily—more, she thought, with an intense weariness, as though with the realisation of the dreadful burden he was having to shoulder. Well, really, if he felt like that about it. . .

'But surely,' she moved her chair half an inch nearer to him and said cajolingly, 'if we can come to some private agreement, no one need ever know.'

'I would know.' He was tight-lipped, as though he could barely trust himself to speak.

'Oh, well.' She made a brave attempt at an insouciant shrug. 'In that case, we're stuck with one another, aren't we? Still, as Jim said, at least it's only for five months.' But Brand did not respond; he merely sat scowling darkly at the table, so she went on, 'Anyway, you'll be going off back to England any day, I suppose.'

That, at least, was one gleam of a silver lining in the dark thunder clouds of the next five months. She had already, even before this had blown up, made up her mind that she would remain out here, for the time being at least, and give herself time to rethink her future.

'No.'

'Oh.' A pause. 'You mean you're staying on in Jamaica?'

Something in her anguished tone must have penetrated the fog of gloomy thought around his head, for he glanced up, scanned her face, then smiled grimly. 'As you yourself so charmingly put it—we're stuck with one another, my dear Fliss. You see, I live out here now—most of the time, at least.'

'You *live* here?'

'Yes.' His tone was perfectly neutral. 'I've bought a house on the road to Frenchy's Bay.'

So he didn't still live at—Sombra.

'Oh, yes, of course, I remember now. That—that day, the first time we met,' again her eyes slid away from his, 'you were talking to Grampy about buying a house here.'

'Yes, that's right. Something like that, anyway,' he replied briefly.

'But I didn't realise. You weren't around when I came back out for Christmas.' Her eyes grew round with horror at the thought that she could have bumped into him in town, on the beach, or even here.

'No.' Again, his tone was totally non-committal. 'I spent Christmas with friends in the States.'

In the centre of the table, Fliss had arranged a bowl of white roses from the bushes which her grandfather had lovingly watered and shaded from the burning heat. In the silence, they both heard a petal drop and Brand absently reached across to pick it up, rolling it over and over between finger and thumb.

Fliss watched until it was completely crushed, then thought, with a spurt of real fear, That's how it'll be with me if I'm not very careful—ground to a pulp. For there was not the slightest hope in her mind now that Brand's guardianship would be an easy ride for her. He'd be rattling his gaoler's keys in her ears morning, noon and night—unless she established her pole position right from day one. That was the answer—get in fast.

She pushed back her chair and stood up, to signify that the conversation was over, then smiled sweetly down at him. 'Of course, I'm afraid that we shan't be seeing much of one another over the next few months. There are things I have to see to here, but then,' she made a snap decision, 'I shall be returning to London—oh, by the middle of next week, I should think,' she wound up airily.

The grey eyes looked up at her, narrowing slightly. 'Sorry, but I've already told you, it doesn't fit in with my plans to go back so soon.'

'I'm not asking *you* to come back,' she pointed out, in her most reasonable tone, 'but you must see that if I'm to pursue my acting career——'

'I'm afraid that your acting career—such as it is——' she shot him a look of pure loathing '—will have to be put on ice for a while. When I said that I didn't intend returning to England yet, I naturally meant that I would not feel free to allow you to either.'

Just for a second, she experienced that same flicker of sheer helpless terror. But it was nonsense. He couldn't possibly prevent her from leaving—this minute, if she chose.

'I don't think you quite heard me,' she said, very distinctly. 'I'm going back to England.'

'Of course you are.' Fliss stared at him, hardly able to believe her ears. 'You're free to go to London, or anywhere else you fancy—after August the twenty-second.'

'I tell you, I'm going next week.' She gripped the back of the chair until her knuckles were white. 'I will go.'

'And I'm telling you, you will not go until I allow you to.' Brand leapt to his feet and they glared at one another across the table.

'And just how do you intend to try and stop me? More bully-boy tricks, I suppose.' Involuntarily, she glanced down at her left wrist and saw the ring of faint shadows from where she had been 'assisted' out of his penthouse and into the cab for Heathrow.

Brand's fists clenched, as though he would dearly love to hurl himself round the table and get a hold of her. She stared fearfully at the dusky red line that flared along his cheekbones. Was she goading him a hair's breadth too far?

Clearly fighting for self-control, he expelled a long breath, then finally said, 'No, by more subtle means actually, this time. After the brief sample I had of your recent—uh—"activities" in London,' at the contemptuous curve of his lip, the mortified colour burned in her cheeks, 'get it into your stubborn little head that I have absolutely no intention of allowing you back there alone. And——'

'And suppose you get it into your stubborn head that——'

'—unless you give me your word that you will not try to leave the island, I shall be forced to request the police to impound your passport—which, of course, as your guardian, I have every right to do.'

Her eyes sparked sapphire fire. 'You wouldn't dare.'

'Try me.'

There was a long silence.

'Well, do I have your word?'

'I suppose so,' she said sullenly. 'You don't really give me any choice, do you?'

He laughed briefly. 'My dear Fliss, I think in my

dealings with you, a choice is the very last thing to give you. So you agree?'

'I've just said—yes, yes, yes.' And after all, she told herself, clutching at consoling straws, small though the island was, it was still large enough to shake him off any time she wanted.

'Good. That's settled, then.'

But, catching sight of her still mutinous face, he went on irritably, 'Now look, Fliss, I didn't ask for this any more than you did. But these next few months; they can be just as easy for you as you care to make them—or as hard.'

At the implicit threat in his words, her eyes flew to his. But then, suddenly, his austere expression softened, he came round the table and stood, regarding her. Before she could draw back, he put his thumb under her chin, tilting her face to his, and gently brushed one finger across the shadows beneath her eyes.

'There are plenty more details to sort out, but not today, I think,' he said quietly. 'I'll go now, unless you want me to stay.'

'No, thank you,' she replied with mechanical politeness, 'I shall be all right.'

He nodded. 'In that case, perhaps we could finalise things over lunch at my place some time?'

'Well. . .'

At her hesitation, he gave a faintly ironic smile. 'Otherwise, we could always meet at a restaurant in town. Maybe you'd be happier on neutral ground?'

Yes, she would. . . On the other hand, though, she felt all at once an intense curiosity to view this house on the Frenchy's Bay road—though only, of course, to see how it compared with the luxurious London penthouse, she told herself quickly.

'No. Your place would be fine—some time.'

'Good. I'll pick you up at noon on Thursday, then.'

So soon? But of course, he was anxious to get this distasteful business over as quickly as possible.

She heard him say something to Maybelle, then a few moments later, the sound of his car starting up. . . 'These next few months. . .as easy for you—or as hard.'

The crushed rose petal still lay on the table. She picked it up, staring down at it in her palm, then hurled it out through the half-open door.

CHAPTER SIX

BRAND arrived before Fliss was quite ready. Tyres crunched over gravel, a car door slammed, then, as her heart pit-a-patted, there were measured footsteps.

She crossed the bedroom, screwing in the dainty hoop earring of plaited silver, and watched at an oblique angle through the slats as he came up the wooden steps. He was wearing dark sunglasses and a long-sleeved black shirt, which somehow made him appear even more than usually intimidating, and a pair of lightweight white trousers, whose cut emphasised the narrow hips and length of leg.

As his shadow fell momentarily across the louvres she stared at him, wanting to hate him—and yet. . . Shocked, she realised that she was watching him with something very like avidity, and turned away quickly, colouring with mortification.

But after all, she thought as she picked up her bag, he *was* an extremely handsome man. Perhaps that was what had originally made him such an arrogant, overbearing swine. Maybe he'd been really nice— well, quite nice—until at around six months old he'd looked in the mirror one morning and realised that he was gazing at a potentially lethal six-foot combination of black hair, chilly grey eyes and. . .

As she pushed open the mesh door, he turned from an apparently rapt study of the hibiscus bush just below the veranda rail, and watched her unsmilingly from behind his sunglasses as she came towards him. Something in the intensity of that regard threatened to undermine at once her already fragile poise, and yet at the same time made her glad that she had taken so much trouble with her appearance for this appointment.

The previous afternoon, having mentally consigned her entire wardrobe to the dustbin, she'd dashed into town to splurge on a new outfit. In an effort to underline that this was a once and for all business lunch, she'd rejected all the loose, shapeless styles which she usually went for, and gone into the shop intent on buying the high-collared navy dress she'd seen in the window. But then she'd spotted, and fallen headlong for this: a linen two-piece, the skirt cut on the bias so that it hugged her hips then flared out to just below her knees, the jacket straight and collarless, and a voile blouse, its softly gathered front falling in snowy folds over her full breasts.

She'd stared at herself for long minutes in the changing-room, gnawing her lip indecisively; but finally she'd managed to convince herself that hot fuchsia-pink looked at least as businesslike as navy, particularly if she coiled her hair into a neat blonde chignon, instead of leaving it casually on her shoulders, as she normally did.

'H-hello, Brand.' She looked up at him, then remembering her vow over breakfast that morning to be on her very best behaviour, she added, 'I'm sorry I'm late.'

He shrugged. 'I was early.'

But he still did not smile and she sensed the tension emanating from him. She could feel it start to swirl around her, and in a bid to shatter it she gave him a teasing pout. 'Oh, dear. You're supposed to say, But it was worth it, you're looking absolutely marvellous.'

His face tightened and he seized her by the shoulders, his fingers digging in as he shook her slightly. 'Don't flirt with me, Fliss. Do you hear me?' His voice was rough. 'Well?' as she did not reply.

'I hear you,' she muttered.

'I won't have you practising your damned repertoire on me.'

She winced as his savage words bruised her inwardly, but only pulled herself clear of him, saying proudly, 'Don't worry, Brand. I wouldn't waste it on you,' then swept past him down the steps.

He opened the car door and she climbed in without looking at him as he slid into his own seat. But then he sat back, tapping the flat of his hands against the steering-wheel.

'Oh, Fliss—how the devil do you do it?' he demanded in an exasperated tone. 'I came here this morning with the best of intentions, and yet within thirty seconds you're provoking me so that I want to put you over my knee and wallop you.'

'Well, of all the unjust——' She choked with outrage. 'I'd have you know, before you arrived, I'd made up my mind to declare a truce—and to keep it up till we can go our separate ways. But then you start straight away insulting me.' Her voice trembled slightly. 'You can't have a one-sided truce, can you?'

'Hmm. A truce until midnight, August the twenty-first? I'm not sure, knowing you, that I can guarantee that.' He shot her a disarming grin. 'But at least we'll say pax for today, shall we?'

What a changeable, infuriating swine he was, she thought resentfully. Nevertheless, she said, 'Yes, all right. Pax.'

'How are you, anyway?' Before she could resist, he had taken the hand which lay nearer to him. 'Are you better?'

'You know,' she said thoughtfully, looking at her slim hand as it lay in his, 'you sounded almost avuncular then—just like Jim Bailey.'

'Well, maybe that's because I also vowed this morning that avuncular was exactly how I was going to be today.' There was a touch of wry humour in his voice, but then he repeated, 'How are you?'

'Oh, much better, thank you. Dr Barrett called yesterday and we had a long talk. He told me that Grampy, at his age, even if he'd recovered, would always have had to be very careful from now on. That would have been terrible for an active man like him— so this way was better.'

He studied her face for several seconds then, as though satisfied, gave a nod and turned away to switch on the ignition.

'I thought you lived out towards Frenchy's Bay?' she asked, as he swung the wheel to turn off the main road.

'I do, but there's a cane lorry overturned. It's chaos further on—and anyway, this is a short cut.'

'But. . .' she began, then hastily lapsed into silence

as the once-familiar narrow road opened up ahead of them and she felt fate's fingers brush bat-like across the nape of her neck, making her skin crawl with tension.

Today, the sugar-cane was not so high, but still there came to her a faint echo, like the faraway sound from a seashell, of that night, of the soft 'putt-putt' of her moped. In another few moments they would be round the bend and then. . .

Her hands clutched convulsively on the strap of her bag and as, against all her volition, her eyes strayed to the distant house among the trees, she heard herself say, in a voice that almost managed to be natural. 'You used to live somewhere round here, didn't you?'

'Yes.'

But far from slowing it seemed to her that he accelerated, not even turning his eyes from the road. . .

'Oh, it's lovely.' As Brand pulled up, Fliss, breaking a silence which had lasted for a long time, sat forward, impulsively clasping her hands. 'What an enchanting house.'

'Thank you. I'm glad you like it,' he said drily, though she sensed that he was pleased. 'It's very old, of course.'

'Has it got a name?'

'Yes, it's called Sandpipers.'

She got out and looked up at the single-storeyed building, set quite alone on a low bluff overlooking a small sliver of creamy sand, between the sea on the one hand and steep, rounded hills on the other. It was large and sprawling, its plain white wooden walls and the long green-painted veranda, which ran the length of two sides, a perfect foil for the riot of shrubs—jasmine, plumbago and bougainvillaea—which covered it.

She turned to him to find his eyes on her. 'Did you plant all those?'

'Afraid not. It was the previous owner, I gather. She was a gardening writer on an American magazine for years, and this was her holiday retreat.'

A Chinese manservant came out on to the veranda, waiting for them, and Brand said, 'Chang, this is Miss Naughton.'

As Fliss smiled, Brand turned to her. 'I expect you'd like to wash your hands. Chang will show you the way.'

The perfect host—urbane and diamond-polished.

'Thank you,' she said in her perfect visitor's manner, and allowed herself to be ushered inside and down a cool passage, where through one half-open door she glimpsed what must be Brand's workplace, with its desk and bank of computers and fax machine.

Chang left her in a small guest suite at the back of the house overlooking the sea. It was a pretty room, the open slatted windows, framed in the white jasmine whose scent hung in the air like delicate smoke, setting off the green and white colour scheme and the simple pale wood furniture.

Everything so spotless, so neat. Chang, presumably—or was it a woman? A woman such as Brand's wife, for example. For the first time ever, the thought leapt into her mind. Was he married? Was he divorced? Did he have a permanent girlfriend? She'd become so accustomed to seeing him, thinking of him, alone—and yet, surely, life's handsome, successful men, who carried around with them that unseen, yet potent sexual aura, somehow didn't look complete in the Sunday gossip pages without an equally highly polished female in tow.

As she washed her hands in the green washbasin, she struggled to put a face to this mythical being. Brand Carradine's Woman. Blonde, redhead, brunette? Tall, willowy, curvy. . .? No, it was no use. The shadow was too elusive for her to bring into focus.

'I thought we'd eat out here.' As she appeared, Brand got up from the swing hammock he was lounging in with legs outstretched, and indicated the table laid for lunch. 'Unless you'd prefer the dining-room?'

'No, this is fine.'

At this far end of the house they were all but poised over the beach, the milky green water sliding softly up the pale sand almost beneath their feet. A small jetty ran out from the beach and a powerful-looking motor boat, with a canopied wheelhouse and elevated rear section—the kind of vessel used by deep-sea sporting fishermen hunting for marlin and shark—was pulled up alongside it.

'Do you fish?'

He followed her gaze. 'Not in that. I use it when I'm diving.'

'Scuba diving, you mean?'

'That's right.'

'Of course, I remember now; that's how you first met Grampy—and ended up getting *landed* with me.'

His lips gave a wry twist and he inclined his head slightly. 'Beautifully put.'

'And you use the boat to get you out to the reef?'

'Sometimes,' he said briefly, then pulled out a chair for her. As she slid into it, Chang appeared with the first course, a salmon terrine, decorated with pistachio nuts and wafer-thin slivers of cucumber. . .

'Mmm. Delicious.' Fliss took up another creamy forkful and popped it into her mouth.

'Chang trained at a five-star hotel in Martinique, so he tends to favour French cuisine.'

'And do you? Prefer French-style cooking, I mean?'

He lifted one shoulder. 'I don't mind what I eat.'

'Oh?'

He caught her look of surprise. 'Should I?'

'Well, I don't know—I would just have thought——' he had removed his sunglasses and she was floundering under the scrutiny from those grey eyes '—that you'd be a man who liked good food. You know——' she paused, but could not resist it '—charbroiled killer whale steaks, or—or medium rare tiger chops.'

He gave her a long, considering look. 'What a very provoking young woman you are,' he said at last.

She was still hunting for a suitably unprovoking rejoinder when Chang returned, and she was able to sit without having to speak while he cleared away with noiseless efficiency, then brought the next course: escalope of veal in cream and Calvados, the rich dish set off perfectly by the plain baby new potatoes and French beans.

'Wine?'

Brand held up the bottle of Reisling, which Chang had set beside him, a faint drift of white smoke rising from its neck.

'Oh, yes, please.'

He filled her glass and his own, then promptly sank into a morose silence, which Fliss found increasingly unnerving.

She swallowed, then heard herself say, in a brittle voice, 'This really is a lovely house. But it's very big—just for one person.'

'Yes, I suppose it is.' He helped himself to more potatoes. 'But you see, Fliss, two people live here.'

'Two?' She stared at him from under her lashes, her knife and fork suspended.

'Chang lives in,' he said smoothly.

'Oh, I see.' Hastily, she reapplied herself to the food in front of her.

'You know, my dear Fliss,' he remarked after a moment's pause, 'for such a devious and complicated young woman——' somehow she kept her gaze on her plate '——you can be remarkably unsubtle. For your information, I'm not married.'

'Oh,' she said slowly. 'I-I wasn't being nosy.' When he gave her a faint smile of patent disbelief she went on more emphatically, 'It's just that—well, with you being my guardian, I ought to know all about you. Of course, I know quite a lot already.'

'Such as?' For a moment, she almost felt the pull of

tension in the air, like a distant violin string very softly twanged.

'Well—that you're a very successful businessman.'

'Is that all?'

'And——' this business lunch was beginning to seem more like a minefield through which she was feeling her way blindfold '—you're keen on scuba diving.'

He laughed. 'Brilliant. Anything else?'

'You've got no children.' She looked straight at him. 'I remember you telling Grampy that.'

'You seem to remember quite a lot about that afternoon.' Across the table, he was gazing directly back at her.

'Yes, I do.' But all at once she found herself unable to meet that challenging look. She took a sip of wine then set down the glass, twiddling with its stem.

When she risked another quick glance, his face had taken on a bleakly forbidding expression. It was as though he had put up a fence between them, as if he was saying, Look, I've had this job foisted on me, and I intend to damn well do my best with it, but don't imagine for one moment that I intend to let you anywhere near me.

He was pouring himself a glass of iced water. She watched as he set down the jug and drank, taking in the hard-edged lines of his face, the strong throat, the way the light, filtering down through the tangle of creepers above their heads, glinted on the black hair, on one strand which lay across his brow. . .

She turned back to her meal again, concentrating

every atom of attention on neatly slicing a tender piece of escalope.

'You know, you've got one earring in higher than the other.'

'What?' Her head jerked up, making the silver hoops swing softly against her cheeks. 'Oh, yes. Well——' she pulled a face '—actually, I pierced them myself, and I didn't quite get the holes lined up.'

'You did *what*?' He stared at her incredulously.

'Oh, yes, it's true. I wanted to have them done— some of my friends had—but it was against the rules of my school. So I got one of Maybelle's big darning needles and. . .' She made a graphic stab at the air with one hand. 'I didn't manage to get them quite level, but no one notices usually.'

Too late she realised that maybe she should have held her runaway tongue. 'Oh, you needn't worry. I'm not like that now,' she assured him earnestly. 'I'm not at all wild, really I'm not.'

'If you say so,' he agreed sardonically. Almost without her noticing, Chang had removed their dishes and now, with a flourish, he set down a chocolate gâteau, its moist dark centre quivering softly, then withdrew.

'You're highly honoured,' Brand remarked. 'He only does his chocolate mousse gâteau for favoured guests.'

'Does he know that I'm your—oh, what's the word. . .?'

'Ward,' he put in drily. 'I haven't told him, but, knowing this place fairly well, I would imagine that the local bush telegraph wires have been humming lately.'

'Yes, so would I.' Rather subdued by that image, she silently took the slice of gâteau he handed her. . .

Chang had set the coffee things on a low table at the far end of the veranda, two basket chairs pulled cosily together. Surreptitiously, Fliss nudged one back a little way with her toe, then sat down rather stiffly.

'Brandy?'

'Oh, no, thanks—I don't really drink much.'

'Good.'

But Brand said it mechanically, as if three quarters of his mind was elsewhere. And there was something else. Today, even here on his own territory, behind his surface urbanity he too was not quite at his ease. There was that slight frown between his level black brows. . .that faint edge to his voice. . .and—she shot him a sidelong glance under cover of picking up her cup—the way he was flicking his coffee spoon against the saucer. Flick, flick, flick.

'Don't you think we ought to have our discussion?' she said, a shade loudly.

'What?' He turned his eyes on her, as though surprised to see her there.

'You know—this is a business lunch.'

'Ah, yes, of course.' He roused himself from whatever dark thoughts had been occupying him and instantly became the incisive businessman again. 'I've talked with Jim Bailey and we've organised everything between us.'

Surely you mean *you've* organised everything, she

thought, but wisely for once stayed silent. Maybe you really are beginning to learn how to handle this one, she told herself ironically.

'He'll pay all your outgoings—the bills for running the house, Maybelle's wages, the gardener, and so on,' he added, as she looked enquiringly at him, 'and you are to receive a monthly allowance, for clothes, et cetera. We thought four hundred dollars would be adequate.'

'Yes, I——'

'And you will be expected to keep within that amount.'

'Oh, I think I shall manage somehow.' Stung by his uncompromising tone, she could not suppress the sarcastic note—although, in fact, she'd been existing on far less for years. 'I have *very* simple tastes.'

'Hmm.' He eyed the fuchsia linen two-piece, which had made such a gaping hole in her bank balance, but then, after a fractional pause, went on, 'And then there's the other matter.'

'My moral welfare, you mean? Oh, don't worry, Brand.' She met his gaze square on. 'I can assure you that you need have no worries on that score.'

'Are you quite sure of that?'

She flared up instantly. 'And what's that supposed to mean, for heaven's sake?'

His mouth curled cynically. 'Well, let's just say that from what I saw of your behaviour in London——'

'Oh!' Somehow, with an instinct for self-preservation, she resisted the impulse to leap out of her chair and punch him. Instead, clenching her hands together in her lap and keeping her voice almost level, she said, 'I've told you, that was the first time I'd ever done a 'gram, and as for the—the way it went wrong, well, you can believe me or not, as you choose.'

'Anyway, be that as it may, that's not all. I don't much care for the sort of company you choose to associate with there.'

'How—how dare you?' She banged her cup down on to the saucer so that it almost cracked. 'Even if you are my guardian—my very temporary guardian, thank heavens,' she amended fiercely. 'You may have hijacked my life for the next five months——'

'Honey, we've both been hijacked,' he interposed grimly.

'—but you've got no right at all to criticise my friends. Lizzie and Deb—they're both really nice. And Al—well, I hardly know him.'

'Then keep it that way.' The overt warning in his voice set her teeth on edge.

'That's up to me—or, at least, it will be, as soon as this ridiculous charade is over.'

'The sooner the better, as far as I'm concerned.'

Oh, it was hopeless. Fliss's slender shoulders sagged wearily. However were they going to get through these five months without tearing each other apart? But there was no point in quarrelling with him. If she gave him the faintest shadow of an excuse, her life really was not going to be worth living. Those one hundred and fifty days would be endless.

How the fates must have been laughing as they'd arranged this ambush, making this man, above all others, responsible for her. But she'd only been telling him the truth when she'd said that he had no need to worry—and it was all thanks to him, she thought with a spurt of bitterness. Since that one night at Sombra she'd never allowed any man to come remotely near her. Those intense, terrifying feelings which had erupted in a blaze of passion had been ruthlessly stamped down until they were grey ashes, dead and cold. They could never be rekindled.

All at once unable to sit still any longer, she drained her coffee-cup and stood up. 'May I have a look at your garden? No—I can go on my own, thank you.' But he was already uncoiling himself from his chair.

'I'm afraid you'll be disappointed.' He was leading her across the coarse grass which surrounded the house. 'My predecessor seems to have spent so much time telling her readers how to run a garden that she never really got round to her own.'

The grounds had certainly been laid out for ease of maintenance, with wide swathes of young cedar and Spanish elm trees, underplanted with oleander and poinciana for colour. More care, though, had gone into the design than was at first apparent, for every few steps made a change of scene, and every vista ended in a glimpse of that glorious blue-green sea.

Slightly ahead of him, she took a winding path through a jungle of crimson-flowered hibiscus bushes, disturbing a flock of tiny blue butterflies, and found herself without warning on the tiled surround of a small oval swimming-pool, entirely enclosed by the hibiscus.

'How pretty.' She turned to him. 'You wouldn't know there was a pool here.'

'I rarely use it. I prefer the sea. But you're welcome to swim here any time you want,' he added casually. 'I know you haven't got a pool.'

'I. . .' she began huskily then froze into silence, one hand at her throat as two images shifted and slid over one another: one of the present, of her swimming in this rippling, sunkissed water; the other, like a faint negative across it, of a dark pool, smooth and opaque like black, midnight marble, and she reaching up towards a statue with a gleaming silvery shell in its stone hands. . .

'If I'm not here, just help yourself.'

What would he think of her, if he ever discovered who she was? The terror that he might one day find out was bubbling inside her. Without waiting for him, she turned and fled blindly, the hibiscus scratching at her arms and legs as she blundered past.

When he caught her up, she was waiting, still pale, by the veranda steps. Without looking at him, she said, 'I'd like to go now, please.' With an awkwardness born of shock, she looked at her watch then lied, 'I-I've just remembered, I promised an old friend I'd call in and see her this afternoon.'

CHAPTER SEVEN

FLISS dropped her beach bag on to the warm sand, stripped off her wrap in heavy lilac cotton to reveal the matching wet-look bikini, and sat down on her straw mat, chin on knuckles, looking idly round her.

The beach was crowded, with the influx of summer visitors reaching its July peak, yet there didn't seem to be a single person she knew, and she heaved a disconsolate little sigh. All her friends from school-days seemed either to have left the island altogether or, like Scott, to be working, and that morning the thought of another endless day alone on the beach, carefully avoiding even casual conversation with any inoffensive young men, just in case Brand might be watching—not that she was in the mood to be chatted up, anyway—had made her spirits droop.

In actual fact, she hadn't even seen much of Brand lately—for which, of course, she was highly grateful. With less than a month to go now, he seemed to be relaxing his iron grip—although, if she was honest, things hadn't been nearly as bad as she'd feared. For one thing, she'd had no difficulty in keeping well within her allowance, so there'd been no painful scenes over what, in any case, was her own money.

There had been just that one incident early on. She'd been sitting in the Admiral Rodney pub one evening with Scott, laughing over school reminiscences, when she'd become aware of a pair of arctic grey eyes watching her over his shoulder. She'd returned look for look, but then, as she'd deliberately turned back to Scott, congratulating herself on freezing Brand out, from the corner of her eye she'd seen him get up, excuse himself to the people he was with—including, she'd noticed resentfully, several extremely glossy young women—and make his way purposefully towards them.

She'd chosen to ignore him right up until a pair of long, jeans-clad legs were brushing against her bare arm as it rested on the chair, then, before she could give him even the briefest acknowledgement, he'd had the nerve to sit down, uninvited, between them.

And not only that—Fliss felt her cheeks turn warm with the memory—he'd wasted no time in reminding anyone who might be within earshot that he was her legal guardian, while she'd been forced to sit there, feeling five years old, a sick smile on her face and just managing to fight off the temptation to slide her steak-knife in between his ribs.

Finally, he had apparently satisfied himself that her companion was harmless—or maybe he'd satisfied himself rather that, whatever Scott's attitude might be, his dutiful ward regarded the young man as no more than a casual friend—and, with a cool nod which encompassed both of them, he'd rejoined his group.

But otherwise, she'd really seen very little of him. In fact, if it wasn't totally impossible, she'd think he'd been actively keeping well clear of her. . .

And yet, she'd always been aware that he was there in the background if she needed him. One minute part of her had found this strangely comforting—and, more than that, was actually going to be sorry when her birthday arrived and he had to set her free.

Oh, come on, Fliss, who are you kidding? she asked herself scornfully. He's an overbearing tyrant and always will be, and, if these last four months have gone so smoothly, it's only because you haven't given him the slightest cause for complaint. Otherwise, he'd have had you in chains and him with the only key before your feet could touch the ground.

But at least he now seemed sufficiently sure of her to be able to leave her alone on the island. Three days ago, he'd rung to say he had to go to New York, then possibly on to Toronto. For a moment, as he'd seemed to hesitate, she'd wondered if he was going to insist that she came too. But then, with a brusque, 'See you,' he'd rung off, leaving her holding the receiver, as a strange tight little ball had formed in her chest. Loneliness, she'd decided later, can play funny tricks on you.

'Fliss. It is you, isn't it?'

A young man was standing over her. Jerked from her thoughts, she stared up at him uncertainly but then, as he grinned down at her, 'Al? Good grief, whatever are you doing here?'

He squatted down on the edge of her beach mat. 'Oh, treating myself to a well-earned vacation. But fitting in a bit of business, as well, of course. I'm out here taking a gander at the local talent.'

'Oh?'

He laughed. 'No, not that. Well, that as well, of course.' He gave her a broad wink. 'But no, I'm touring the night spots, taking in the cabarets—hoping to turn up the next Bob Marley.'

'Any luck yet?'

'One or two, maybe, that I can talk contracts with. But I'm still looking. Have you any ideas?'

She shook her head slowly. 'No, sorry. I can't think of anyone.'

'But surely you're in touch with the local scene. You've been out here—what?—four months now.' There was a slight pause. 'By the way, I heard about your good—I mean,' he pulled himself up smoothly, 'your sad news.'

Of course. She'd written to Lizzie with just the bare facts of her grandfather's death and her inheritance, and saying that she wouldn't be returning to London—just yet. Pride had not permitted her to reveal exactly *why* she wasn't coming back, or that a guardian had been appointed. Or who that guardian was. . .

'You're looking very fetching, Fliss.'

Al's eyes swept appreciatively over her tanned body, taking in the curve of her breasts, her tiny waist, the seductive line of her lips, so that she made a faint involuntary move as if to reach for her wrap.

He saw the movement and gave a boyish laugh. 'Oh, don't mind me, darling. I'm so used to giving lovely women the once over—purely in the line of duty, of course—I do it automatically.'

And he said it so frankly that she had to laugh too, and relaxed a little.

He glanced down at his watch. 'Look, do me a favour, Fliss—have lunch with me. I've discovered this great little seafood restaurant in town.' When the doubt must have shown in her eyes, he added cajolingly, 'I hate eating alone.'

'Well.' She still hesitated, eyeing him from behind her sunglasses. True, in his beach trunks and flowered shirt he seemed much nicer somehow than in those ultra-sharp city suits. But even so—what would Brand say? She swallowed at the appalling thought and found herself actually half looking over her shoulder, but then thought defiantly, Oh, what the heck? It's only lunch, and it's a shame for anyone to be on holiday on their own. And besides—the sneaky thought dropped in—Brand is several thousand miles away, isn't he?

She smiled up at him. 'Thank you, Al. That would be lovely.'

'Thanks for your company, Fliss.'

'Oh, I enjoyed it.' And she had. Over lunch, Al had proved an amusing companion, filling her in with a series of hair-raising anecdotes on all the latest antics of Deb, Lizzie and the others. 'Well, if I don't see you before you leave. . .' she went on uncertainly. They were strolling along the picturesque if slightly seedy old waterfront beneath the tall warehouses where once tobacco, sugar-cane—and slaves—had changed hands.

'Are you going back to the beach?'

'Oh, no, the afternoon's too hot for me. And besides, I'm going out tonight.'

'I'll run you home, then.' And, taking her arm, Al steered her firmly towards his hire car.

As he drew up outside the house, Fliss got out, but before she could begin her goodbyes he had climbed out too.

'So this is your place.' He was looking around him with frank interest.

'Yes. My grandfather left it to me.'

'Lucky Fliss. A nice little piece of real estate, this.'

She smiled at him uncertainly. 'Thank you for bringing me home. It saved me a broiling walk.' Then, as he showed no signs of leaving, she added politely, 'Would you like to come in for a drink?'

She led the way up the steps to the veranda and pulled up a basket chair for him. As he sat down, he said casually, 'Look, about that little spot of business I mentioned over lunch. The show's an absolute winner—all it needs is another backer, and with your——'

'No, I'm sorry, Al,' she put in firmly. 'I would never sell this house—I love it too much. And as for my money, well, as I told you it's rather tied up at the moment.' Though something still kept her reticent about precisely how.

'Pity. Ah, well,' he shrugged, 'if you change your mind, you know where I am.'

She gave him a non-committal smile. 'Now, what would you like to drink? Lime juice, or——' she added quickly as he grimaced '—white rum, or I think there's some imported Scotch.'

'That'll be fine, thanks. With ice.'

Leaving him with his feet up on the rail, she went

through to the kitchen and poured a whisky and a tall glass of lime juice for herself. She tipped out the contents of a packet of pretzels on to a plate, then picked up the tray. As she was going back down the passage, though, she paused. Her wrap was really hot and under it, in spite of the shower she'd had at the beach, the straps of her bikini were chafing her shoulders where sand had penetrated.

A quick glance through the shutters showed her Al, leaning back, eyes closed. She hurried through to her bedroom, put down the tray on a bedside table, then pulled a light cream cotton smock dress out of the wardrobe. She went on into her tiny shower-room, dragging off the beach top as she went, and dropped it on to the floor, followed rapidly by her bikini.

A half-minute shower was all she dared allow herself, then, snatching up a bath towel, she went back through to her bedroom, hurriedly blotting at her body, and walked straight into Al.

With a stifled cry she jerked back, bringing the towel up in front of her, but his arms went round her and he was dragging her to him.

'Fliss, darling——'

'No, no! Let me go!' she cried. '*Please*,' in stark terror, as she caught sight of his face, flushed with sudden desire.

He released one arm, but only to strip the towel brutally from her clutching fingers; then, his hands dragging into her shoulders, he held her away from him. She could feel the heat of his eyes burning her as they travelled across her bare flesh.

'God, what a body,' he muttered thickly, then as, with a whimpered protest, she began to struggle, 'Come on, honey. You know you want it as much as I do.'

'No! I said let me go!'

'Let you go? Not just yet, my sweet. But if you'd rather have it this way. . .'

She heard his laugh, the laugh of a man triumphant in his conquest, and with a strength born of desperation she brought her arms down sharply, slackening his grip momentarily, and turned to escape. But, scarcely able to see for blind panic, she stumbled against a chair and before she could recover Al had pounced on her.

Catching her round the waist, he flung her down on to the bed. As she lay helpless, all the breath knocked from her, he came down beside her, pinioning both her wrists and thrusting one knee across her thighs. Oh, why didn't Maybelle hear? Fliss, desperately twisting her head on the pillow, opened her mouth to scream but at the same instant, as Al clamped his hand over it, she remembered with a sickening jolt of her stomach that it was the housekeeper's afternoon off. There was no one to rescue her.

'Come on, Flissy—relax.' Against her breast, his voice was hoarse. 'I'll make it good for you, I promise.'

Her eyes closed, she felt him fumbling with the catch of his trunks and braced herself for one supreme, futile effort to save herself. But then, miraculously, his weight was off her.

'What the hell——?'

Dimly, she heard his exclamation of surprise then, a split second later, an animal-like grunt of pain, and when she opened her eyes she saw through her tangled hair Al being lifted clean off his feet, exactly as he had done to her just moments before. Brand was holding him at arm's length, like a gyrating puppet, and smashing punches one after another into his unprotected face until she saw a red rose of blood flower on his upper lip and his right eye close.

In this state, Brand might do anything! Careless of her nakedness in her real terror for him, she leapt up from the bed. '*No*, Brand! Leave him. You-you'll kill him!'

She seized hold of his arm but, his face still contorted with fury, he shook her off. Her intervention had defused his anger slightly though, and after one final blow he stopped, letting Al hang helplessly away from him.

'She might even be right.' His lip curled in a contemptuous sneer. 'And you're not worth swinging for.'

Half carrying, half dragging Al across the room, he disappeared through the door. Fliss took one step after them but then, as dizziness flooded through her, she gave a faint cry and sank down on to the bed, the room reeling around her.

'Cover yourself up.'

She was unaware that Brand had returned until she heard his voice. As she gazed blankly at him he snatched up the smock dress, throwing it at her, and gratefully she pulled it down over her head, dragging her hair clear with unsteady hands. When she looked up again he was staring out of the shutters, his back turned to her, and the fixed rigidity of that back terrified her almost more than Al's assault had done.

'Brand, I . . .' she began shakily, then broke off abruptly as he turned slowly to face her. He regarded her for long minutes, and his expression made her very heart tremble.

'What do you want?' he asked stonily.

What did she want? She wanted him to take her in his arms, as he had when Grampy died, to soothe away the fear, tell her that she was safe now; but as he deliberately crossed the room and stood gazing down at her, bleak-eyed, she knew that comfort was the very last thing she was going to be given this time.

Behind that pale mask and cold grey eyes he was very, very angry. She'd never seen him so angry, and her spirit, already flayed by Al's attack, cringed away from any confrontation. All she could do was look at him silently, mechanically brushing a dishevelled skein of hair from her forehead, then all at once she put her knuckles to her mouth.

'What's the matter with you?'

I want you to hold me close to you. 'I-I feel sick.'

'A common symptom, my dear—of thwarted sexual desire.' His voice was like the light flick of a whip curling across a raw wound, and she flinched. 'You know, you almost had me fooled.'

'W-what do you mean?' she whispered.

'What do I mean?'

Without warning, the frozen façade cracked; he

took a couple of steps towards her and, putting his hand under her chin, forced her face up. His knuckles were split across—she saw the traces of blood on them, then seconds later felt it sticky against her own skin.

'Tell me, Fliss. How have you survived these last four months? Well?' He gave her head a savage jerk when she did not reply.

'I-I don't understand you, Brand.' Her voice broke on the last word.

'And then, the second I'm safely off the island. . . Or maybe you didn't even have to survive,' he went on, as though half to himself. 'Maybe, while I thought you were behaving yourself, you were just being too clever for me. Is that it? Sneaking around like a bitch on heat, but taking very good care to cover your tracks.'

The horrible picture he was conjuring up at last penetrated her dazed mind. 'Oh, no——' She stared up at him imploringly. 'No, It isn't true, Brand. I swear it.'

'Oh, those beautiful innocent eyes.' His mouth twisted. 'Don't swear anything—you don't want to add perjury to your list of misdemeanours, do you?'

He was killing her inside, but somehow she had to stand up to him, make him see that she was wholly innocent.

'Brand.' Leaping from the bed, she clutched at his arm. 'It isn't how it looked when you arrived—you must believe me.'

When he continued to freeze her with those chipped-ice eyes, she shook his arm urgently. 'I met

Al by chance on the beach. He asked me to lunch, and as I was l-lonely,' her voice stumbled on the word, 'I agreed. When he brought me home, I offered him a drink, and. . .' She trailed off miserably, her eyes darkening at that remembered scene.

'And of course you make a habit of serving drinks in your bedroom,' he jerked his head savagely to where the incriminating tray still stood on the table, 'at three in the afternoon, naked. Unless, of course, you preferred to have Al strip you. With the whisky as a little liquid refreshment for—afterwards.'

'No.' She spoke through lips stiff with fear. 'You've got it all wrong. I only came in here for a quick shower.'

But even in her own ears her voice lacked conviction. Oh, what was the good? Whatever she said, Brand would never believe her. Still, though, if only for the sake of her own pride in herself, she had to make him hear the truth.

'You must believe what you wish,' she said woodenly. 'But however it looked, I am innocent.'

'You know, my sweet,' he was continuing as though she had not even spoken, 'I told you in London that you weren't fit to be out on your own. But maybe I got it wrong.' He paused. 'Maybe it's the men who need protecting when you're around.'

'Oh.' Through the grey, numbing fog of misery which was threatening to overwhelm her, the merciful anger came, cold and clear. 'How dare you?'

Her right hand went back and she slapped him hard across the cheek. It was a dull, dead little sound, and for a moment after it there was an intense silence, apart from her rapid breathing. She saw Brand's skin grow white under the stinging blow, then dark red, and as his eyes narrowed his hands clenched at his sides.

Terrified of what she might have unleashed, she made a wild spring for the door. She reached it, slammed it in his face, then threw herself across the veranda, down the steps and into the garden. If she could once reach the overgrown thicket of shrubs which surrounded the rough lawn, she would be safe in hideaways still remembered from childhood.

But, even as she plunged into a tangle of bamboo stems, she was seized roughly from behind. Choking for breath, she could not speak, and Brand, ignoring all her frantic stuggles as though she were no more than a small bird trapped in his hands, hoisted her over his shoulder, carried her back across the lawn and dumped her in the passenger seat of his car. He flung himself in beside her, breathing hard, and she saw with a stab of fear that she'd managed to tear two buttons off his beautiful white silk shirt, leaving ragged holes.

Without a word, without even a glance in her direction, he snapped on the ignition, slammed the car into gear and shot off down the drive in a flurry of gravel. Once out on the narrow road, he jammed down the accelerator even harder, then, as the verge flashed past at a speed which left Fliss weak with terror, he snatched up the car phone and punched out a number.

'Brand Carradine here. Can I speak to Jim Bailey. . .? Well, when he gets back give him a

message, please. Tell him I've got my—ward. . .yes,
Felicia Naughton, with me. Oh, and would he send
someone to the house to lock up in case the housekeeper's late getting back?'

Crackling squawks came from the phone, which he
cut through with an impatient, 'Yes, that's right.
She'll be away from home tonight.' Then he hung up.

Away from home tonight? What on earth was he
planning to do with her? He'd kidnapped her before,
of course, and that time she'd ended up first in his
penthouse apartment and then five thousand miles
away out here. . . They were following the Frenchy's
Bay road, so presumably they were heading for
Sandpipers.

'I suppose you're planning on keeping me locked
up in chains on bread and water in your cellar,' she
muttered resentfully.

'I don't have a cellar—unfortunately.' He did not
take his eyes off the road.

At the house he reached for his jacket, which lay
on the rear seat, and got out. By the time she too,
after waiting as long as she dared, had climbed out,
he had unloaded two cases from the boot. Fliss stared
at them. He must have come straight to her house
from the airport—it was almost as though he'd
actively *wanted* to catch her out in some misdeed, she
thought, her lips tightening on an unexpectedly
vicious stab of pain.

Chang had appeared and she managed a pallid
smile for him—after all, it wasn't his fault if his
employer was the biggest bullying rat on the island—
then watched as Brand handed him the cases and

said something in a low tone which she could not catch.

When she went to follow them up the steps, he turned back to her. 'Wait here. And I do not recommend that you try to run away again.'

'Really?'

She held his gaze with what she hoped was a challenging stare, but as he swung away her shoulders drooped. She looked around her half-heartedly, as though assessing a means of escape, but it was no use. She simply did not dare move and, what was more, he knew that she didn't.

Five minute later, when Brand came back, she was leaning morosely against the car, her arms hugged across her chest. He had changed into a white cotton shirt, but had not even taken the time to button it up and it was tucked roughly into the waist of his denim shorts. Barely glancing at her, he said curtly, 'This way,' and led her towards the beach.

The paved path led down a rough flight of steps to the small jetty, where the motor boat was still moored. Brand jumped down into it then turned to her.

'In you get.'

She stared down at him. 'What are you *doing*?'

'What does it look like? We're going for a ride.'

'We most certainly——'

'Get in—or I drag you in feet first.'

As she still hovered, her toes curling on the edge of the concrete, he reached up for one of her hands and gave her a smart tug which brought her down, first on to a slatted seat, then stumbling on to the deck beside him. She fell heavily against him, but, before she could do more than register that hard, unyielding body through the thin material of her dress, he had thrust her away from him, setting her down on the bench.

She leaned back against the rail, watching as he switched on the motor and reversed slowly away from the jetty into clear water. As he spun the wheel and opened the throttle to full, the boat leapt for the open sea, the green waves hissing under the pointed prow.

The wind pressed her against the seat, ripping the breath from her mouth, snatching at her hair. She reached down automatically for a scarf from her bag, then remembered—no scarf, no bag. Nothing. Not even bra and pants—just the cream cotton smock dress.

Feeling the warmth creep up into her face, she tucked the dress more firmly under her thighs. No shoes either. For the first time, she became aware of her dusty feet, criss-crossed with scratches from when she had run away from him.

Her eyes strayed upwards to the man standing at the controls. The wind was whipping at his unbuttoned shirt so that, by just craning forward a little, she could see the whorls of tiny black hairs on his chest, glistening in the low sun, and the firm ridges of stomach muscle beneath the brown satin-smooth skin.

All at once, she felt rising in her an almost irresistible urge to get up and move across to him, to lay her head on that strong, comforting chest and weep out of her the tears of shock and self-pity that hovered

just beneath her surface calm. But then her gaze rose
to his granite-edged jaw, the tightly compressed line
of his lips as he stared fixedly ahead, and she too
turned her eyes to the distant horizon.

Ahead of them now, a small islet had appeared—
one of the uninhabited cays off the coast, no doubt.
Gradually, the indistinct shadow turned to a line of
greenery and a slim, palm-fringed curve of beach,
and as they crossed the barrier of white-surfed reef
Fliss realised first that there was a makeshift landing
stage, and second that they were making rapidly for
it.

Brand cut the engine and they cruised in alongside,
then he threw a rope and, leaping out, secured it to a
wooden bollard.

'Right. Out.'

'Here? But you said we were having a ride.'

'You've had your ride. Now—get out.'

Bridling at his peremptory tone, for a moment she
toyed with the idea of defying him, of saying 'No' and
continuing to sit there, but then as, grim-faced, he
made a threatening move towards her, she scrambled
out and reluctantly followed him along the uneven
planking and on to the hot white sand.

Without a glance at her, he set off up the beach
but Fliss hung back. There was something so *purpose-
ful*, a kind of silent intensity about him. . .

Even as the faint *frisson* of unease ran through her,
he turned. 'Come on.' His voice was still snap-edged,
as though he could barely trust himself to speak to
her.

'No, I won't.' She dug her toes into the sand. 'I

swear I won't budge from this spot until you tell me what the h-hell's going on.'

She could not restrain the betraying tremor of fear in the last words as he came slowly back to her and stood regarding her, his black brows knit, and—her eyes dilated—the mark of her fingers, pale but still plainly visible against the dark flush on his cheekbone.

'What's going on?' she repeated as he did not speak. 'And why——' she glanced around her, hearing only the silence '——have you brought me here?'

He shrugged. 'I needed somewhere for tonight, while I decide what to do with you—and this seemed as good a place as any.'

'But you've absolutely no right——'

'Why not? It's my island.'

'What?' Her jaw dropped in disbelief. 'You mean—you *own* it?'

He smiled grimly. 'How quickly you catch on, when you really try.'

'But—but you've never said.'

'Why should I?' His eyes were two silver-grey flints. 'You've chosen not to tell me everything about your—affairs.'

'Now, look here——'

'And you can count yourself highly privileged, my dear Fliss. I don't normally tell people of its existence, let alone bring them out here. But, in your case, I've made an exception.'

'Well—that's big of you.'

'Be quiet.'

Although he spoke the two words very softly, it was

the voice he'd used on Laslo and on Al, and she immediately fell silent, contenting herself with scowling at him. No man had *ever* spoken to her—treated her—the way he did. Men were always charming to her, pleasant, indulgent. Even Al, until that terrible scene in her bedroom, had been far nicer than this— this overbearing brute would ever learn how to be.

'As I said,' he went on, his quiet voice still holding that thread of menace, 'you're staying here tonight, while I decide what's the best thing to do with you.'

'Tonight? No, wait.' Obviously irritated, he was turning away, but she'd suddenly remembered something. 'You can't keep me here tonight. I've got a date.'

'Well.' His mouth twisted into a sneer. 'You'll just have to let Al down again, won't you?'

'No!' It was only fear that kept her from striking him again. 'Not with him. I've *never* had a date with him, although I don't expect you to believe that. If you must know, it's with Scott.'

'Well, you'll just have to stand him up, won't you?'

'I'm not hearing this.' Her voice rose shrilly. 'I suppose it's your idea of punishing me—dumping me here all alone tonight.' Her eyes strayed to the dark line of trees and undergrowth fringing the sand, the long shadows reaching down the beach almost to where they were standing, and she fought a shudder. 'You know what? You're some kind of—of twisted masochist.'

'I think you've got the wrong word, honey. Surely you mean sadist?'

'That as well,' she retorted hotly.

'But you see, you won't be here all alone. I'm staying too.'

Aghast, she could only stare at him; then, 'But—but you can't.'

'Can't I?' He gave a short, humourless laugh. 'It seems to me you need reminding of something. You're still my ward—for just three more weeks, thank God—and if a guardian discovers his ward to be in grave moral danger——'

'I wasn't——' she began, though with little real conviction.

'—he has every right under the law to do what he considers necessary to protect her—if necessary, from herself.'

Far more than all his high-handedness, the sheer injustice of his words seared her, so that she could have crumpled to the sand at his feet, But, on top of all her other humiliations at his hands, she would not give him that gratification. Instead, she straightened her shoulders, setting her head proudly. If he always chose to think the worst of her—well, let him.

'Yes, you're quite right, Brand.' Summoning all her acting abilities, she injected a sultry throb into her voice. 'I did invite Al back to my house, and of course I wanted him to make love to me. And then *you* had to arrive.'

Through the terror that her own provocative words were creating in her, she had the small, bitter satisfaction of seeing the suspicion on his face change to a thunderous scowl.

'Well?' as he looked at her in silence. 'Will that do?

After all, it's surely what you want me to say. That's the way you want to think of me, isn't it?'

Her breath caught on the final words and she saw his face whiten, his hands clench into fists, but then he turned on his heel and walked past her up the beach.

CHAPTER EIGHT

FLISS stood watching Brand, one hand to her throat, until he had disappeared among the trees, then she plumped down on to the beach, hugging her knees, her chin on her arms. But almost at once, in too much of a turmoil to remain still, she leapt to her feet and began pacing up and down, up and down, scuffing up the sand with her toes in angry little spurts.

The sun was setting. As she watched, its red-gold rim slid down below the horizon, and instantly the sea went leaden grey. On the land, dusk was swallowing the trees and from among them came soft, surreptitious rustlings. Rats? Or was it gigantic land crabs, emerging from their burrows like pallid ghosts? No, it was much more likely to be a flock of kling-kling birds, settling down to roost for the night—wasn't it?

The rustlings came again and she forced down the panic which was flaring in her. She couldn't possibly stay here on the beach alone. And yet—how could she bear to follow Brand, laying her bruised spirit open to even more of his savage taunts?

A despairing tear rolled down the side of her nose and as she brushed it away a small shape scuttled out from among the rotting timbers of the jetty to disappear into the darkness.

'Brand!' With a stifled cry, she ran headlong up

the beach, stumbling along the path which he had taken.

She broke through a clump of almond trees and saw, on a small plateau overlooking the sea, a single-storeyed house of white weather-boarding. There was no sign of Brand, but she went up the wooden steps to the porch and tentatively pushed open the mesh door.

It led directly into a large sitting-room, basically furnished with wood-framed sofa and chairs draped with ethnic-style blankets in soft, earthy colours, and a large glass-topped bamboo coffee-table. Black and rust Mexican rugs lay on the polished floor, and a pair of abstract seascapes hung on the wall. As she stood there, looking around her, she became aware of a low humming noise coming through the open window. The generator, presumably, which supplied the electric power on this out-of-the-way spot—but the sound merely added to the overall impression of tranquillity.

At the far end of the room was a single door. She was staring at that one door, weighing up its possible implications, when she heard movements from behind it. Hesitantly, she opened it and found herself in a kitchen, complete with cooker and large fridge-freezer. Brand had its door open and was taking out two steaks.

'How do you like yours done?' He didn't turn— eyes in the back of his head, on top of everything else, she thought.

'I don't want——' she began, but then, as he favoured her with a swift frown, 'Well done.'

'Set the table, will you? It's out on the veranda. You'll find the things in here.'

He gestured to a wall-cupboard then turned back to the freezer and took from it half a dozen bread rolls, a small pack of peas and another of baby corn cobs. When he glanced over his shoulder, she had not moved.

'Didn't you hear me?'

'Yes.' She smiled unsweetly at him. 'Ask me properly.'

He muttered something which she was glad she didn't catch, then, 'Will you set the table—*please*?'

'There you are. It didn't hurt too much, did it?' she said, and went across to the cupboard. . .

'Mmm.'

Fliss pushed away her empty plate then, looking up, caught what just might have been a glint of amusement in Brand's eyes. 'A sea voyage always gives me an appetite,' she said frostily. 'But anyway, I suppose I should be grateful you don't intend starving me into submission.'

'I don't somehow think that anything as crude as starvation would work on you.'

He took the plates and came back with a wicker basket of fruit, which he set down beside her.

'Mangoes. Lovely. Are there trees here?'

'Several. Some were already here when I bought the island, and I've planted more, as well as some Chinese bananas and a lime. There's also an old ackee tree, which I've never been brave enough to try.'

'No, well, you've got to be very careful with ackees,' she said seriously. 'They're lovely, but if you don't know what you're doing you can easily be poisoned. I could——'

She broke off and, taking a large mango from the basket, hastily began peeling back the rosy skin to reveal its honey-sweet flesh. She had been about to say, 'I could show you tomorrow, because Maybelle taught me,' but she wouldn't be here tomorrow. And anyway, the thought of Brand flat out, legs in the air—only temporarily, of course—after a feast of badly prepared ackee was quite a cheering one.

'You like mangoes?' Brand remarked and Fliss, her teeth sunk into a juicy fruit, glanced up at him then followed his eyes down to the pile of stones on her plate.

She pulled a face. 'Yes, I do. They're my favourite, but——'

'Don't worry. There are plenty more.'

'Of course——' all her attention was on a shining trail of juice trickling down her wrist, which she was catching with the tip of her tongue, and she spoke without thinking '—out here, people say that the only way to enjoy mangoes properly is to eat them in the bath. I often do at home.'

At the image her words conjured up, she stopped with a little gasp, staring across the table over her head. Brand too was looking at her, his pale grey eyes, through some trick of the light, very dark suddenly.

'Why did you buy this island?' She blurted out the first thing that came into her head.

'For solitude.' His voice was expressionless. She thought of him, sitting out here, his legs stretched out in front of him, gazing out at the sea—dazzling, beautiful but empty—and her heart pinched suddenly with a feeling which was almost pity. And yet, she told herself fiercely, a man like Brand didn't need anyone's pity. If he was solitary, then that was the way he'd chosen it—*wanted* it. After all, that was how he'd been when he first came out here, wasn't it—the way he'd lived at Sombra? Like some crazy recluse, or something. . .

'And also because I'm keen on diving, and the coral reef around this cay is superb.' He paused. 'That's the main reason I'd called on your grandfather that day—it was his advice which made me decide on this place. He's the only person who's ever stayed out here with me. Until tonight, that is,' he added in a wholly neutral tone, as she glanced up at him quickly from under her lashes.

He reached for a juicy ortanique, then went on. 'I've taken up underwater photography the last couple of years, and I'm planning a TV series on the reef—that's why I went up to New York—and a book to go with it. Oh, don't worry,' he went on quickly. 'It won't displace your grandfather's—nothing could ever do that. But I hope, in a way, it'll complement his work.'

'I see,' she said slowly, then her generous mouth curved into a smile. 'I'm sure he'd be glad, Brand. He liked you very much.'

'Yes—well.' To her astonishment, she saw his lips

tighten as though she'd said something unpalatable, then abruptly he pushed back his chair. 'Coffee?'

But the curt rebuff he'd just given her little olive branch was too painful. 'N-no, thank you.' She turned her head away so that he shouldn't see the sheen of tears in her eyes. 'I'll wash up, and then I'd like to go to bed. I'm very tired.'

As she put her hand on the nearest plate, though, he pulled her wrist away. 'Leave it. I'll do it later.'

As they'd sat talking over their fruit in what was the nearest they'd ever got to a companionable manner, to her astonishment she'd found herself half hoping that he would suggest they did the dishes together. But, of course, in reality he was as anxious to be rid of her company as she was to be away from him.

She followed him into the kitchen, then Brand opened a door and flicked a light switch.

'This is my room. Yours is through here.' He pushed open another door, revealing a bathroom. 'We share this, and you'll have to come in and out through my room, I'm afraid.'

'Oh, don't apologise.' Her nerve-ends were twitching, making her snappy. How could she ever hope to sleep so near him, with just this small bathroom between them? 'After all, it means I can't *possibly* escape, so you can be sure of a good night's sleep.'

'That's true.' But he sounded as though he was barely listening. 'Through here.' He switched on a bedside light and she saw that they were in a narrow room, just large enough for a bed, with a mosquito net bunched above it, and a chest of drawers. He turned away as though to go.

'No. Wait, please.' As he came back, slowly, she said, her tone still slightly waspish, 'I seem to have mislaid my luggage. Can you possibly find me something to sleep in?'

His eyes flicked just once to the cream smock dress. 'If you need to sleep in anything, use that.'

'No, I won't,' she said indignantly. 'You may not care how I look, but I do. And I refuse to go back to Kingston tomorrow looking as though I've been dragged through half a dozen hedges backwards. This is creased enough already—look.'

She held handfuls of cotton away from her body then, remembering that underneath she was totally naked, let the dress fall back, her face flaming.

'I sleep in the raw myself.' The picture which Brand's laconic words conjured up—that lean, beautifully proportioned body clad only in the satin of his skin—hit her like a physical blow somewhere below the stomach. 'But if you insist. . .' Putting up his hands, he began to unbutton his shirt.

'No, I couldn't possibly——' She broke off in confusion as he held it out to her.

'It's this or nothing.'

'Well—all right,' she said reluctantly, but then, as she moved across to take it from him, she winced suddenly.

'What's the matter?'

'Oh, nothing. It's just that I scratched my foot down on the beach—I must have trodden on a shell or something.'

'Let's have a look at it.'

'No. It's nothing—really.'

'Sit on the bed and let me see.'

As she unwillingly obeyed, he knelt in front of her, taking hold of her foot between his hands, then began probing gently—so gently that she did not flinch—at the torn skin on the instep, where blood was still seeping slightly.

'How the hell did you do this?' He sounded almost angry.

'Oh, something frightened me—a rat, I think—when you left me on the beach. I-I was running to find you.'

'What a child you are.'

He looked up at her, their faces just inches away from each other, her lips parted tremulously. Just for a moment, something flickered in his sombre face, then he put down her foot and stood up.

'I'll get some antiseptic cream.'

'Really, there's no need. . .' she began, but he was already in the bathroom.

She heard him rummaging around in the cabinet, running water, then he was back with a small bowl and a wad of cotton wool. Ignoring her protests, he knelt down again and began bathing the injured foot.

She leaned back slightly, looking down at him, absorbed in his task. The rosy light from the bedside lamp gleamed on his tanned chest and shoulders and gave his face an impression of softness which in daylight it did not possess. The habitual chill grey of his eyes was hidden; all she could see was the shadow cast by his lashes lying across his cheekbones, while from this angle his mouth, drawn thin from years of too many cynical, caustic remarks, had about it a wholly deceptive sensitivity.

If only this was the real Brand Carradine. . . Suddenly, without warning, Fliss found herself aching to cradle him to her breast, to caress that dark head and make that illusion of tenderness a reality. Had any woman ever done that? Could any woman ever do that? Perhaps—but it would never be her, she thought, and felt that knife edge of pain turn sharply in her guts again.

He must have felt the tremor which ran through her, for his fingers stilled for an instant, then he said, 'I think that's it.' Setting her foot down he stood up, then, without looking at her, added, 'I've put out a toothbrush for you, and a towel.'

'Thank you, Brand.' But she spoke the soft words to the door panel as it closed behind him.

Fliss sat for a long time, staring into nothing, then, rousing herself, tiptoed through to the bathroom. No light showed from under his door—he must be in the other part of the house still. She washed quickly then returned to her room and took off the smock dress, hanging it up carefully from a hook behind the door.

She picked up the shirt and held it against her; it still felt warm from his body and she could smell very faintly the mingled aroma of sweat and aftershave. That touch, those scents, were all at once strangely disturbing and she quickly did up the tiny pearl buttons, jumped into bed then pulled down the mosquito net around her.

Switching off the light, she lay in the warm darkness. Wrapped in Brand's shirt, the subtle, musky odour weaving itself around her nostrils, it was, she thought, as she drifted easily into sleep, almost as though she were being held safely in his arms. . .

When she appeared on the veranda next morning, Brand was already sitting at the table, a coffee-pot at his elbow and a dish of hot rolls and fluffy cassava cakes, butter and some pale logwood honey in front of him.

'Good morning.' Carefully averting her gaze from his bare chest and shoulders, Fliss slid into the chair opposite him.

He grunted something which just might have been, 'Morning,' but did not look up and continued making notes in the file beside him. Pursing her lips, she fought down the spurt of irritability. She'd surprised herself by sleeping well, had woken feeling amazingly happy and relaxed, and come out here determined to show Brand that she really did have a good side. For this morning, at least, sulks were things of the past. But now, as he took a morose sip of coffee, and continued with his notes, she felt her ebullient mood begin to falter slightly.

'How's your foot?' At last he broke the silence, but still did not raise his eyes to her.

'Oh, fine, thank you. It doesn't hurt at all.'

She poured herself a drink and took a cassava cake, spreading it with butter and honey. Still without glancing up, he tore off a sheet of paper and pushed it across to her, together with a pen.

'What's this for?' She stared at him blankly.

'Make a list.'

'A list? What on earth are you talking about?'

'Clothes, toiletries—anything else you'll need from your house. And any shopping, of course.'

She gaped at him, horrified, then said in a strangled voice, 'You mean—you're not taking me home today?'

'That's right.'

'But—but where are you taking me, then?'

'Nowhere. You're staying right here.'

'I'm not!' She leapt to her feet. 'I'm going back with you this morning—now!'

'Sorry, but you're not.' For the first time that morning he looked directly at her. 'You can't be trusted on the mainland, so——'

'Don't talk such rubbish. Of course I can be trusted. Oh, why won't you listen to me?' She banged her hand on the table, so hard that the cups and plates clattered.

'Do your list.' He pointed a long finger at the paper. 'Or I'll just have to get Maybelle to sort out anything she can.'

She stared down at the top of his head, as he turned back to his own writing. For two pins, she'd snatch up that file and beat him senseless with it. Her fingers balled into fists at her sides but then, with more self-control than she'd ever known she possessed, she forced herself to drop into her chair. Argument was useless. If she'd learned one thing, very painfully, about Brand Carradine, it was that everything—*everything*—went his way. The world bent itself around him, to accommodate him, as he strode through it, and no exceptions could be tolerated.

As she drew the paper towards her, she said very distinctly, 'Can I get just one thing straight? How long are you planning on keeping me here?'

'Until August the twenty-second.'

'And after that?'

He looked straight at her. 'After that you're free—to do as you please.'

Her fingers tightened again for an instant, but she made herself go on, her voice icy calm. 'And you'll be staying here as well, I presume.'

'Naturally. I wouldn't put it past you to try something brainless like swimming for Venezuala if I'm not here to keep you under control.'

Fliss gulped down the panic. She'd coped—just—with yesterday, but to be out here alone with Brand for another twenty-three days—and nights. . .

Picking up the pen, she rapidly began scribbling and after a few minutes thrust the carefully folded sheet at him. Opening it, he read, 'Bras, pants, nighties——'

'All right, all right! There's no need to read it out loud. I wrote it—remember?'

He re-folded it and slid it into the pocket of his shorts, then glanced down at the slim gold watch on his wrist. 'I should be back by midday.'

'Great,' she snarled. 'I really look forward to that.'

The grey eyes regarded her for a moment. 'Oh, by the way, I forgot the washing-up last night. Do it, will you—*please*?'

Last night she'd have done it—if not happily,

willingly enough. Particularly—crazy as it seemed now—if he'd been beside her, helping. Again, at the picture, there came that sudden squeeze inside her, and to kill the pain she yelled, 'No, I won't!' and, to make her intention quite clear, she snatched up the dish of rolls and cassava cakes and threw it across the table. It hurtled past Brand's right ear and landed on the grass behind him, scattering its contents in all directions.

In the silence that followed she heard, above the palpitating of her heart, Brand expel a long, slow breath.

'That was a pretty infantile thing to do,' he said at last.

It was. She hadn't had a temper tantrum like that for years. But it wasn't fair—she really had been trying and *he* had brought out all her latent, futile aggression.

'You know something, Brand Carradine?' He had torn off the sheet he'd been writing on and was now getting to his feet. 'I hate you—I *really* hate you.'

He gave her one brief, glinting glance. 'I can live with that.'

'Yes, well—I suppose you're used to it.' But the feeble retort bounced off his back as he headed off towards the beach.

Having gathered up the dishes—as she'd known all along she would—she carried them through to the kitchen and dumped them in the sink, then began scrubbing them within an inch of their lives. Her face was still flushed with temper but, as she put the last plate into the cupboard, she remembered Brand's expression as the dish whistled past him, and her lips twitched.

But at once the smile faded. 'You're a fool,' she told herself aloud. 'He's a dangerous man—Loretta sensed that, years ago, and you've seen at close quarters how he can react when his anger's roused. So, for heaven's sake, stop provoking him, otherwise. . .' She ran the tip of her tongue around her lips, which had suddenly gone ash-dry.

With a violent gesture, she upended the washing-up bowl, then, thrusting her feet into an old pair of flip-flops—miles too large—by the kitchen door, went outside to explore her prison.

CHAPTER NINE

THREE hours later, having made so many complete circuits of the tiny cay that she'd lost count, Fliss was beginning to know every piece of driftwood, every grain of sand. She'd first explored the orchard behind the house, where Brand's fruit trees were thriving, then, taking a handful of mangoes, she'd wandered along the shoreline, splashing through the warm shallows, heedlessly bedraggling the skirt of her dress, as she ate the scented fruit.

She'd seen the double row of footprints still in the sand from yesterday and there beside them was a single line, heading seawards, where Brand had trodden today. Stepping in his footprints, she'd followed them to the jetty, which looked almost stark now without the motor boat tied up alongside it; then, with a curious empty feeling inside her, she'd walked on along the beach.

At the far side of the island she'd discovered, among the twisted, slimy roots of mangrove, a tumble-down shack at the water's edge. The door had fallen off its hinges as she'd touched it, and when she'd peered in she'd seen in the far corner a dug-out, the kind of boat the local fishermen used. Probably they'd built the hut as well, as a refuge for the times when fierce north winds blew down from the Atlantic, turning the translucent sea into grey froth.

She'd studied the dug-out thoughtfully for several minutes. Brand had said she was quite capable of swimming for Venezuela—well, maybe this could at least get her as far as the mainland. It looked very rickety though. . . Before she dared entrust herself to it, she'd have to be a lot more desperate to get away from him than she was already. And anyway, knowing her luck, before she was halfway there she'd meet him coming back. . .

The sun was almost overhead now, and the heat out here on the beach was almost unbearable. If only she dared cool off with a swim. She hesitated, shading her eyes to peer out to the horizon, but no boat was visible; so, stripping off her dress, she waded out into the clear water and struck out in a fast crawl before turning over to float on her back, her eyes screwed up against the sun.

It really was a beautiful islet; a tiny, unspoilt gem. If she was going to be kept prisoner anywhere, well, there could hardly be a lovelier dungeon on earth. Paradise—with just one enormous fly in the ointment. . .

If only she hadn't thrown that dish. It had been a childish fit of temper, which would just have confirmed Brand's minimal opinion of her. But he wasn't going to let her go anyway, so why should she care in the slightest what he thought of her? But she did. With painful clarity, she knew suddenly that she cared very much. I'll show him, she resolved. In three weeks, I'll show him that I'm not a spoilt baby, and when that blissful day comes and he lets me go——

But all at once, there was no pleasure in that

thought—rather, a dull, heavy feeling under her ribs.
What on earth was the matter with her? Surely, the
first second that cage door opened, she'd be out
through it like a bat out of hell—wouldn't she?

A faint sound broke in even as the appalling doubt
began to form, and turning her head she saw the
boat, quite close in, heading purposefully for the
shore. With a faint gasp, she tore through the shallows, snatched up her dress and retreated behind
some oleander bushes to drag it on over her wet body.

By the time she arrived at the jetty, Brand was
unloading two cases which she recognised as hers,
another case and some boxes. At first he did not see
her, and she stood watching as he humped out the
luggage, totally engrossed in what he was doing. The
old denim shorts which he had on were moulded
tightly to his flat abdomen and thighs, and the
muscles in his deeply tanned shoulders and arms
rippled under the silky skin.

As she watched him she knew all at once, with a
terrible sick certainty, why it was that it was going to
be so hard for her to break free from him. On that
forbidden night at Sombra, in almost the same instant
that her womanhood had burst into joyous flower, it
had been crushed. For nearly five years, she had
existed in a dry barren desert, but now, in that split
second, she realised that her body was aching for
Brand to take her in his arms again. She wanted him!

Her blood was thrumming in her ears, so loudly
that she thought he must hear it. She moved restlessly
on the sand and as Brand bent to pick up a case he

saw her. For a moment, he stopped dead, then slowly straightened up.

'Come and give me a hand.'

But when she scrambled up on to the jetty, he stood regarding her, taking in her bare feet, her streaming hair, and—she saw his glance with pleasure now—where her dress had curled itself to her damp body. Behind his sunglasses his face was inscrutable, but she sensed the tension in him as, rather stiffly, he lifted one hand and, taking up a strand of wet hair which lay across her cheek, tucked it behind her ear.

'You look like a drowned mermaid.' His voice was husky.

'Mermaids can't drown.' It was a breathy little whisper.

He stood motionless for a moment, his hand against the side of her face, then he abruptly dropped it.

'If you take that case, I'll bring these up,' he said tersely, and picked up a box.

Fliss poured herself another cup of coffee and sat sipping it as she gazed across at the sparkling sea. Another beautiful day—another glorious, thoroughly *boring* day. Behind her, as her heart performed its usual morning pitter-patter, she heard Brand's footsteps, then he dropped into the chair opposite.

'Morning,' she said brightly, though without quite looking at him, and received a grunt in return. 'Coffee?'

Another grunt.

She poured the coffee and a glass of orange juice, which she'd just squeezed, and pushed them across to him, together with a plate of croissants that she'd heated from frozen earlier.

'Thanks.' He caught her eye and gave a half-apologetic grimace. 'Sleep well?'

'Yes, thank you.'

In fact, she couldn't remember a time when she'd slept better. She dropped off each night, lulled by the shush-shush of the sea curling up to the beach, and even if she woke it was somehow very comforting to hear, through the thin partitions, Brand turning over in bed—even sometimes, she fancied, his steady breathing. But he wasn't sleeping half so well, she thought, studying him over the rim of her cup. There were dark shadows under his eyes, and that ever-present tautness round his mouth.

'What are you doing today?' she asked.

'Diving, of course.' He glanced up. 'And what's wrong with that, for heaven's sake?'

'You dived all day yesterday, and the day before that, and the—in fact,' her voice shook slightly, 'you've done nothing but dive for the last sixteen days, and then shut yourself away each evening writing up your notes.'

'Now, don't start that again.' He put down his cup with an impatient thump. 'I've *told* you. I haven't been able to give my attention to diving for months, for various reasons,' he shot her a meaning look, 'and I'm way behind schedule.'

'But what am I supposed to do all day?'

He rolled his eyes in a 'give me patience'

expression. 'You can sunbathe, swim—people pay a small fortune to do just that out here. You can read.'

'I've read every book Maybelle sent out for me at least twice, and all yours too.'

'Well,' he looked around for inspiration, 'you could always practise your singing.'

'My what?' She gaped at him.

'I heard you the other evening.' His lips quirked slightly. 'I seem to remember you were doing the washing-up at the time.'

'I'm sure I wasn't,' she protested. 'I never sing— well, only in the bath.'

'Well, maybe that's where you were then. Anyway, it sounded pretty good to me. No, really,' as she looked at him suspiciously. 'You've got quite a voice there. Have you ever auditioned for musicals?'

'Well, no,' she said uncertainly. 'I've always gone for straight acting parts.'

'Think about it, then. See what's coming up when you get back to London.' He paused. 'You will be going back to London, I presume?'

'Oh, yes, of course,' she replied, hoping that she sounded more confident than she felt. In fact, with only a week to go now, she still had no idea what she was going to do.

'Well, there you are, then.' The day was settled to his satisfaction. 'Borrow some of my tapes and sing along with them.'

'I don't want to.' She jutted her lower lip mutinously. 'I want to come diving with you.'

He muttered something inaudible. 'And don't start that again either.'

'I know you've got some spare wet-suits. That red one fits me perfectly. Not that I've tried it on, of course,' she added hastily.

'*No.*'

'Well, just take me out in the boat with you. I'll be very good, I promise.'

'Oh, yes, I'm sure.' He laughed grimly. 'Leave you alone on the boat, complete with the ignition keys? You'd be off over the horizon before I was halfway down to the reef.'

Tears stung her eyes. He didn't want her with him; he was just making excuses. The bitter pill of truth was that he simply couldn't stand her anywhere near him. She was an unavoidable nuisance, coming between him and his solitude. It was ironic, really— she wanted to be with him more and more, while he. . .

As he drained his coffee-cup and stood up, she raised her eyes, some demon of self-destructiveness luring her helplessly on.

'*Please*, Brand. I promise I'll——'

'And I promise you,' he cut in brutally, 'that if you know what's good for you, you won't say one more word about diving.' And, turning on his heel, he strode off in the direction of the beach.

Fliss sat quite still. She'd done it again—in spite of all her best intentions, she'd provoked his anger. She tapped one finger miserably against the table edge. For the past two and a half weeks, she'd really tried: she'd cooked nice meals for him, kept the house tidy, never—until now—allowed herself any sulks or fits of temper—though heaven knew she'd been provoked enough.

And through it all, in a funny kind of way, she'd actually enjoyed the challenge of self-discipline she'd set herself. But what had she got in return? Most of the time, he all but ignored her, making it obvious that he preferred his room to her company. And all the time, parallel with their alternate spats and polite, brittle conversations, was the undercurrent of her feelings for him, which she had struggled against so hard.

Suppose she betrayed herself to him? Suppose, one day, he surprised her watching him, as she found herself doing more and more? And worst of all, suppose something—her voice, a gesture—betrayed to him who she was? Of course, it would only confirm his view of her, merely reinforce his contempt. But she—how could she bear that? She had to get away— now—before it was disastrously too late.

She got up precipitately, ran through to her bedroom and threw a few belongings into her straw beach bag, then stumbled headlong down the steps and across the cay to the fishermen's hut. Heaving for breath, she lugged the dug-out to the water's edge. It grated against a sunken mangrove root then floated clear.

She scrambled aboard, picked up the wide-bladed paddle and launched herself in the direction of the indistinct blurs on the horizon which were the mountain tops of Jamaica. . .

* * *

The sweat was dripping into her eyes. She wiped the back of her hand across her face, then, dropping the paddle, straightened her aching back. Her arms and shoulders felt as though they had been racked from their sockets and she flexed them gingerly. When she was little, she'd sometimes gone out with Maybelle's two nephews, conch fishing in their canoe, but then they'd just indulged her wish to row for five minutes. Now, it was all down to her.

As she bent to grip the paddle again, she saw out of the corner of her eye a motor boat, the prow slicing a 'V' of white foam as it skimmed the water. Next moment she let out a groan of horrified disbelief. It *couldn't* be—he was fifty feet down, swimming lazily among the coral. But she was already paddling frantically, head down, for the shore.

Now he had found her, Brand seemed in no hurry. He slackened speed and began cruising round her like a prowling shark, wide at first, then moving in for the kill in tighter and tighter circles. At last, he cut the engine and drifted alongside, until his hull nudged gently against the dug-out. It rolled slightly and Fliss, who had been determinedly staring at the horizon, clutched at the sides.

'And where might you be off to?'

When she darted an upward glance, Brand was looking down at her, his elbows propped on the rail.

'For a mid-morning row. What else?' She gave him a defiant look.

'What else, indeed?' he agreed gravely, though there was a glint in his eyes.

'So if you'll just get out of my way, I'll be getting on.' At least she was still trying.

He straightened up and held out his hand. 'Let's have that bag.'

Mutely, she handed it up, then, as he stretched out his hand again, allowed herself to be hauled up into the boat, to be deposited ignominiously among his diving gear.

'What about the canoe?' She had to shout above the sudden roar, as he restarted the engine.

'Leave it. You won't be needing it again.'

She watched listlessly as the now-familiar outline of the cay rose in front of them, and when Brand coasted in alongside the jetty she remained sitting silently. He put his hand under her elbows and lifted her to her feet, but then stood still, holding her, as she studied a tiny snag in his navy T-shirt.

'I suppose you're going to lock me up in the house from now on?' Her voice quivered as, suddenly, she felt very weary of all the cat and mouse games they'd played.

'I might do just that.' He smiled briefly but his voice was sombre, and there was a strange expression in his eyes, an expression which made her heart flutter madly.

'H-how did you know I'd gone?'

'No idea. I just had a feeling—maybe I'm developing a sixth sense as far as you're concerned.' All at once, he grabbed hold of her shoulders and shook her fiercely. 'Why the hell did you do such a damn fool thing? You realise you could have drowned?'

Her eyes skittered past his. He must never guess

why she had felt that sudden, overwhelming need to get away.

'I-I was cross, because you won't take me diving with you. Oh, why won't you, Brand?'

'I won't take you,' his face was set, 'because I daren't.'

'Daren't?'

'Scuba diving is a highly dangerous sport——'

'Well, I know that. . .' she began indignantly.

'—and you're just not to be trusted. I don't trust you as far as I can see you on dry land. And a hundred feet down, well. . .' He shrugged expressively, then, when she said nothing, he went on, his voice softening slightly, 'I'm sorry, Fliss, but you're just so immature. I mean—look at the crazy way you've behaved this morning.'

'But that was only——'

'You're still a child, Fliss. And the sea-bed is no place for a spoilt, wilful child.'

'No, Brand, you're wrong!' she burst out. 'I'm *not* a child—I'm a woman. I-I mean, at least,' she felt herself colouring confusedly, 'as far as diving is concerned, I am. Grampy started taking me when I was ten, and I couldn't have had a better teacher. I know all about buddy diving—how you've got to obey your partner without question or you'll both be in serious trouble. I promise you, I would never, ever do anything stupid down there. But of course,' she blinked back the sudden, infuriating tears that were pricking her eyes again, 'I don't expect *you* to believe that.'

For long moments he looked at her without speaking; then at last he stepped across on to the jetty and held out his hand to her.

'Come on. Let's see if we can find you that red wet-suit.'

She gaped up at him, her heart gyrating. 'You mean——?'

'That's right—buddy.' He gave her a wry little smile. 'We're going diving.'

Fliss gave the thumb-and-finger 'OK' sign, rolled backwards off the side of the boat and kicked downwards to drift effortlessly through the clear water.

Inside the face mask, her eyes widened as she reached the topmost points of coral. This section of the reef was less than thirty feet beneath the surface, so visibility was clear—they wouldn't need the powerful torch which Brand had taken down with him on that marvellous night dive a couple of evenings ago—and yet, just as he'd promised, it must be by far the best she'd ever seen.

Just ahead of her were tall red coral spurs. They looked soft and spongy, yet when she brushed her hand across the top of one, it was rock-hard. Beyond them was an outcrop, looking like an enormous desert cactus, while to her left lay a carpet of velvety blue fan corals, with shoals of brilliantly coloured fish weaving in and out among them.

She was trying to break off one of the fans, a small, perfectly shaped one, when Brand, in his black wet-suit, swam up alongside her and pushed her hands out of the way. Sliding out the knife which he wore strapped to his thigh, he cut through the base and handed it to her.

Fumbling with the opening of the collecting bag she was wearing at her waist, she slid the fan in and closed it, just as another shoal of scarlet and gold fish shimmered past, like warm rain pelting softly against her outspread fingers.

She was swimming along the side of a coral cliff when, in front of her, in a cleft, she saw the blunt head of a moray eel moving gently in the current. It looked like a really big one, much larger than any she'd seen before, but as she moved towards it Brand put his hand on her arm, giving her a peremptory 'No' sign with his other palm.

He glanced at his watch and, tapping it, jerked his thumb upwards. Oh, no—it couldn't possibly be time to go up already. Through her mask, she gave him a beseeching look, but then nodded, returned his thumbs-up signal and obediently followed him back to the safety line before kicking for the surface, a trail of bubbles floating up ahead of her.

Brand helped her into the boat then closed her regulator valve and lifted the air cylinder off her back. She peeled away her face mask.

'Oh, Brand, it was marvellous—the best yet. Can we come back here tomorrow?'

She was unhitching the weights belt from round her waist, and looked up, her face glowing, but he only said, 'Glad you enjoyed it,' and turned away.

'Here, let me do it.'

She put up her hands to help him off with his cylinder, but he said curtly, 'I can manage, thanks.'

Fliss bit her lip; some of the champagne sparkle of the dive was fading already. But she mustn't let it. After all, she knew well enough by now what a moody, changeable man he was. Sometimes, these last five days since they'd started diving together, he'd been a friendly, warm companion; at other times, for no reason that she could see, he would retreat into himself, like that hermit crab she'd been gently teasing down on the beach this morning.

Only yesterday afternoon, as they had gone to the house from their dive, they'd been laughing together over the way he'd seized a huge passing turtle and hitched a ride for several yards before finally releasing it to paddle indignantly away.

Almost without thinking, it seemed, he'd put his arm across her shoulder, and, just as unthinkingly she'd laid her head on it. Next moment, though, he'd withdrawn his arm, badly jerking her neck, and walked quickly away up the beach. When she'd reached the house, he'd already shut himself away, writing up the day's log.

And today, right from breakfast time, he'd been silent, withdrawn—morose, even. But he mustn't spoil today. After all, there was only tomorrow, and then. . .

Brand had removed his wet-suit, to reveal his dark navy trunks, and quickly she began peeling herself down to her lilac bikini. The last few days she'd become accustomed to being in it alongside Brand. Usually, she felt faintly self-conscious in any sort of swim gear, but far from ogling her as most men did, so that she could almost feel their sweaty fingers pawing at her flesh, right from the start Brand had seemed completely oblivious to the full, rich curves of her body.

The first couple of days she'd found his total lack of interest in her somehow disturbing, but then, telling herself that she was being stupid and childish, she'd decided that it was all to the good. Since her abortive attempt to escape, she'd struggled really hard to subdue that treacherous feeling of attraction for him, and if he still saw her merely as that most dreaded of beings—a ward—well, that was entirely for the best.

Squatting down on the deck, she tipped out the contents of her collecting bag, poring over them: an empty sea urchin shell, several small pieces of Neptune's brain coral, and the lovely blue fan.

'It's gorgeous.' She stroked one finger over it, then without thinking, held it up in front of her face, looking at Brand over the top, her lashes fluttering, a coquettish smile curving her lips. But, when he gazed blankly back at her, she dropped the fan to the deck.

'Good grief.' She gave a strained laugh. 'For a moment I thought I was back in drama school. We did a class once, where we had to improvise with fans. You know—try and create all sorts of different moods and situations without using any words. . .'

Confusedly, she bent to pick up a large, crusted oyster shell, and Brand gave a groan. 'Oh, no, not another of those things. I've told you, you don't get pearls out here.'

'Oh, please open it. I really think this might have one.'

She managed an almost natural smile and, reaching across for his knife, he inserted the point of the blade, twisted it and split the shell into two halves. Taking them, she prodded at the contents.

'No, nothing,' she said mournfully. 'But look, the mother-of-pearl is really beautiful.' She held it for him to see, stroking gently across the silvery interior. 'Oh, it's the exact shade of your eyes. I-I mean——' she looked hastily down at the shell again '—I'd love it as a necklace. Could you make a hole in it for me, please?'

Without a word, Brand took it and, as he put the knife point to the whorled end of the shell, she leaned forward, untying the sodden scrap of black velvet ribbon with which she'd restrained her hair during the dive. When, still without speaking, he handed back the shell, she threaded the ribbon through it then tried to knot the ends at the back.

But her wet hair was in the way. She knelt down, her back to him, fumbling ineffectually with the ribbon, then felt him take both ends from her, his warm fingers making the skin at her nape tingle as he lifted her hair out of the way and tied a knot. He turned her round, still kneeling, to face him and looked down at the shell.

'Keep still. It's twisted.'

He caught hold of it and gave a little tug, which set it swinging free between her breasts. As he released it, she felt his fingers very softly brush against the curve of one breast and gasped with shock as it tautened in immediate response, the sensation rippling instantly outwards through her whole body, setting every pulse-beat throbbing, every nerve-ending quivering with delicious longings.

She jerked away, forgetting she was on her knees, and fell heavily against him. He steadied her, and for a moment she lay in his arms, feeling the slow drag of damp bare skin against bare skin, and the strong beat of his heart under her shoulder. As they stared at each other, the slanting sun broke through a low cloud bank on the horizon, turning their faces and bodies to bronze. She was so close to him that she could see the tiny lines etched at the side of his mouth, his silvery grey eyes, rimmed with charcoal, the irises black as night.

Just for one moment, something blazed up in those eyes, then he muttered brusquely, 'Time to go,' and thrust her roughly away from him. Huddled on the bench seat, Fliss watched as he swung the boat round then drove hard for shore, as though a pack of sea demons were at his heels.

He ran the boat in beside the jetty, rasping it against the timbers, then, without turning, said harshly, 'Go and get your things.'

'My. . .?' She frowned in bewilderment.

'Get your things,' he repeated impatiently.

'Whatever for?'

'I'm taking you back to the mainland.'

She got up slowly and crossed the deck to stand beside him. The sun had set, draining the gold from their faces.

'But—why, Brand?' she faltered.

'Because it suits me not to keep you here any longer,' he said brutally. 'I'm letting you go two days early. Well?' as she stared blindly at him. 'That's what you want, isn't it?'

She stood quite still, not looking at anything, then, in a voice she barely recognised as her own, said, 'Yes, of course that's what I want, Brand. I'll go and get my things.'

CHAPTER TEN

'ARE you quite sure that's what you want, Fliss?' Jim Bailey looked across his desk at her, his brow furrowed.

'Quite sure, Jim,' she said firmly. 'I've thought about it a lot these last—three weeks.'

Her glance slid away from his. This was the first time either of them had made even the most oblique reference to her sudden disappearance, and equally sudden return. 'I've made up my mind. I don't want to have all of Grampy's money—I'll keep enough to tide me over the next few months, but I'm going to make my own way in the world.'

'Hmm.' The lawyer's mouth pursed doubtfully. 'Well, I know that Sue will be very grateful—she'll be able to set up that Boy's Club in downtown Kingston that she's been trying to get going. But have you—er——' he fidgeted with his pens '—discussed all this with Brand? After all, he is your guardian.'

'No, he's not.' Again, she did not quite meet his eyes. 'Not since midnight last night, he isn't.'

'And have you decided what you're going to do, now you've come of age? Will you stay on here, or are you going back to London?'

'Well, no, I haven't really made up my mind,' she said evasively. 'But there's plenty of time for that.'

'Perhaps you *ought* to talk to Brand.'

'No!' Abruptly, Fliss pushed back her chair and stood up. Talk to Brand? When he had so cruelly thrust her away from him? Oh, when they'd got back to the marina, he'd insisted on getting her a cab to take her home, but then he'd manoeuvred the boat away, without even a glance over his shoulder, and roared off as though he couldn't bear to be with her one second longer.

She picked up the small jewel box from the desk. 'Thank you again for the locket. It's really lovely.'

Jim, too, had got to his feet, but he seemed reluctant to let her go. 'How are you spending the rest of your birthday?'

'Oh, you know.' She gave him a bright smile. 'I'll probably go down to the Admiral Rodney this evening. Some of the gang are sure to be there.'

'Well, you know that Sue and I would be delighted if you came up to Prospect Hill. Or how about us taking you to the Trade Winds? Their meals are really excellent.'

'That's very kind of you both.' Unexpectedly, Fliss found her eyes burning with tears and she blinked them quickly away. 'But you mustn't worry about me—I'll be fine.'

After the chill of Jim's air-conditioned office, the heat outside was stifling. She wandered into the dusty main square, shimmering under the afternoon glare, and stood irresolute. She really might as well go home—there was no one around, apart from a few tourists, clutching their souvenirs from the local craft market and now making their way back to their cruise ship.

But the thought of the house, silent except for Maybelle's cheerful singing, was somehow repellent to her in her present mood, and instead she went on down through the narrow streets towards the waterfront. When she reached the Admiral Rodney, she stood for a few moments, looking up at the inn sign creaking gently in the hot breeze from the mountains—the sign which Scott had been in such trouble over when he'd 'borrowed' it as his dare that night. . . 'If you're really uptight about Sombra—I don't mind changing with you.'. . . If only—if only she had. . .

She wandered restlessly along the waterfront, then leaned against the rough stone wall, looking down at the row of battered fishing-boats and at a group of men, among them surely—yes, Maybelle's two nephews, who had taken her out with them all those years ago. They were crouched in the shade of some scrubby dogwood trees, their low voices lilting in the island patois as they prepared their nets for the night's fishing.

It was a picturesque scene, yet for once Fliss was blind to it. For she knew now how it was that she would spend the rest of her birthday. . .

She put down the hair-drier then looked at herself in the dressing-table mirror. Usually, she left her blonde hair loose on her shoulders, but tonight she'd decided she wanted it piled up in a more sophisticated style. It was a struggle, but finally the mass of hair was subdued into a smooth knot, just two silky strands left to frame her face.

Standing up, she unhitched the towel she had wrapped round herself then slowly surveyed her body—rounded, gleaming from the lotion she had just smoothed on to it, and deeply tanned, except for the two bikini marks and that silvery little heart shape on her thigh. Heart shape. . .

She stared into her eyes a moment longer, then, as though terrified at what she glimpsed in those dark blue depths, she turned away, quickly putting on her bra and pants. Again, she hesitated, looking down at the dress which lay on the bed, but then caught it up. Sugar-pink, its raw silk flowed over her body like cool water, its gentle scoop neck setting off her head and shoulders, its straight lines emphasising the high swell of her breasts, her slender waist, and the feminine curves of her hips.

No jewellery, she decided, except for the slim gold bangle her grandfather had given her for Christmas—anything else would distract from the shimmering simplicity of the dress. No make-up either—just the merest slick of lip gloss. As she replaced the top, she looked straight at herself again. There was a soft flush on her cheeks; her eyes were dark, like huge brilliant sapphires; and round her soft mouth hovered a tremulous, almost wistful look.

She stared at herself a moment longer, feeling her courage drain away. But then, whirling round, she pushed her feet into flat white sandals, picked up the small supermarket bag, and went through to the kitchen.

'I'm off now, Maybelle.'

The housekeeper took her in her arms and hugged her. 'Bye, my honey—have a lovely birthday.' Her voice brimmed with emotion, and Fliss kissed her.

'Don't wait up for me. I can let myself in.'

There was one last swish of the oars, then the boat grated on the sand and Fliss, gathering her things, jumped out.

'Thank you.'

The two young men, their faces glinting in the light of the full moon, regarded her doubtfully. 'You sure you all right, Miss Fliss?'

'Yes, I'll be fine, Errol.'

'Aunt Belle—she skin us and boil us for this,' said the other man lugubriously.

Fliss laughed, more lightly than she felt. 'She'll never know, I promise. And I'll find my own way back.'

She stood on the sand, watching as the boat glided silently away, until the big, bobbing lamp at the stern had faded to a spark from a match, then bent to slip on her sandals. Find her own way back? She'd probably be back in Kingston before they'd caught their first crawfish. What a terrible risk she'd taken, coming back here—risking his fury that she should dare to disobey him. And even now that she was here she didn't know why she'd come; only that, finally, she'd had to, as though something outside herself was driving her.

As she walked quickly up the beach a strange feeling, half fear, but the other half wild elation, was running like quicksilver through her veins, so that she found herself panting for breath.

In the shadow of the trees she stood looking at the house, bathed in moonlight, her ears strained for the slightest sound. But the house was dark, silent. He must have closed up and left. She bit on her lip, the desolation welling up inside her, and walked slowly forward. And then, at the corner of the house, she halted abruptly.

Brand was there. He was leaning back in an old basket chair on the veranda, a book discarded and lying open on the low table beside him. One arm was thrown behind his head, casting an intense shadow over his face so that she could not make out his features, but she sensed him staring out into the darkness.

And then, without the least warning, she knew. Knew why she'd never looked at another man— Scott, her fellow students, Al. . .they'd all barely existed for her; why she'd been happier than she'd ever been in her life those last magical days—and why she'd come back here tonight, like a fragile moth fluttering helplessly towards a flame.

But love, surely, was ushered in with bells and trumpets and people throwing flowers. That was what she'd always believed—it wasn't born from anger and resentment and loathing. And yet. . .with every fibre of her being, she loved Brand.

The knowledge was so terrible that she turned as though to run, but that tiny movement roused him. He turned his head sharply, went to get up out of his chair, then for a moment froze before slowly straightening up.

'Fliss—is that you?' His voice sounded shaken, quite unlike his usual hard, confident tones.

'Yes.' It came out as a croak, but after the tremendous shock she was surprised she could speak at all, astonished that she could calmly walk towards him.

He stayed on the top of the veranda steps, the moonlight on his face, until she stopped one step below him.

'Why have you come back?' His tone was empty of all expression.

She'd rehearsed this moment fifty times in that boat, how she'd say carelessly, 'Oh, there's no one around back home. All my friends are away, and I didn't fancy being on my own this evening.'

Instead, she said, 'I wanted to spend my birthday evening with you.'

A spasm of what looked like anger flickered across his saturnine face, and for one anguished second she thought he was going to take hold of her and march her back down to his boat.

But he said, 'Have you eaten?'

'N-no. But it doesn't——'

'I went fishing this morning.' His voice was still constrained, as though he was holding himself on a very tight leash. 'I caught two lobsters. Will that suit you?'

'Oh, yes, perfect. And, because it's my birthday, I've brought this.' From the supermarket bag, she took out a bottle of champagne and hesitantly held it out to him.

'I'll put it on ice,' he said brusquely and led the way to the kitchen, flicking on the light switch. . .

'More coffee?'

'No, thank you.' Fliss pushed her cup and saucer away. 'And thank you for a lovely birthday meal, Brand.'

He did not quite return her glance. 'Not exactly a fancy one, I'm afraid.'

'Freshly caught grilled lobster, salad and a basketful of mangoes straight from the tree. What could possibly be better?'

He gave her a faint smile, the first that evening, then picked up the glass of champagne which had sat beside his plate virtually untouched.

'Happy birthday, Fliss,' he said formally. 'And everything you want in the future. That's what's said on such occasions, I believe.'

'Yes.' She touched his glass with her own, sipped a little, then set it down, pushing it round and round in tiny circles. She shouldn't have come, of course. She'd been crazy even to think of thrusting herself on him tonight, when he'd made it so crystal-clear he wanted to have nothing more to do with her.

If she'd stayed away, she could still have held on to some shreds of wounded pride. As it was, the tension between them all through the meal had set her nerve-ends jangling, while Brand's constrained manner—hardly looking at her, his hand moving sharply away when it had accidentally brushed against hers as they'd both reached towards the fruit basket—had put a terrible chill in her heart. The sooner she was back on the mainland the better.

'Well—I'll wash up, then,' she said in a brittle voice.

'Certainly not.' He smiled almost naturally at her, the corners of his eyes crinkling, and that smile made her cold heart ache. 'No young woman washes up on her twenty-first birthday in my house.'

He had changed before the meal, into close-fitting black canvas jeans and an open-neck white shirt, which set off his deep tan in the candlelight. Suddenly, she couldn't sit there any longer opposite him, in terror that he would read in her eyes the truth about her feelings, and scorn her for them. She pushed back her chair.

'It-it's such a lovely evening. Can we go for a walk along the beach—before you take me back?'

'All right,' he said, the reluctance all too obvious. 'You go on. I'll catch you up.'

As he disappeared into the house, Fliss stared out into the warm darkness, tapping the champagne cork against the table. She should never have come back. . . Slowly, she got up and began clearing the dishes away.

She picked up her half-full glass, put it to her lips, then on an impulse hurled the champagne into the bushes beside the veranda, did the same for Brand's, then finally snatched up the bottle from its ice bed and poured it all out.

There was no sound. He wouldn't come after her, of course. It would be like so many other evenings when she'd sat here alone, or trailed off along the beach, seeing the light pouring out from the living-room, and Brand in there, sitting at his desk, staring at the opposite wall.

The small portable tape-recorder which had accompanied her on so many solitary night walks still stood by the window, where she'd put it that last afternoon. Suddenly afraid of the silence that was waiting for her outside, she caught it up then went off towards the beach.

She wandered along aimlessly but then, sitting down on the sand still warm from the day's heat, she switched on the tape and stared, bleak-eyed, at the little waves, their crests glittering in the light from the full tropical moon, as they ran up to her toes. But gradually, the music began to permeate her brain. It was the last tape she'd used—orchestral arrange-ments of famous movie themes. Lush, sentimental; but they had somehow matched her mood then, and now the sensuous sweep of violins playing 'Love is a Many Splendoured Thing' all at once broke through the wall of glass she'd built around herself the last two days.

She bit down hard on the soft inside of her mouth as the empty desolation washed through her, but then, too tense to sit still, leapt to her feet and took a few tentative dance-steps on the water's edge. Trying to blot out all her feelings, she let the music take her over completely and began moving more freely, sway-ing rhythmically, dancing out into the wavelets themselves.

As the last notes died away she dropped her hands to her sides and turned, to see Brand, watching her.

She stood quite still as he came towards her, the tension once more vibrating in the air all round them. In the moonlight, his eyes gleamed as silver as the slim package he was holding out to her.

'Happy birthday, Fliss.'

She slid her thumbnail under the edge and pulled back the paper to reveal a black, oblong box. Inside, nestling in white satin, was a long rope of pearls.

Trembling slightly, she lifted them out, letting them trickle through her fingers like a string of pale, opalescent fire. Over them, she stared up at Brand.

'Are they real?' There was awe in her voice.

'Of course. I was going to send them on to you, but now that you're here. . .'

Send, not give.

'I can't possibly accept them, Brand.'

'Of course you can,' he said harshly, but then caught himself up and gave her a crooked little smile. 'You were always hunting for pearls out on the reef, weren't you?'

'Thank you, Brand. They're beautiful.' She in turn almost managed a smile, then held them out to him. 'Will you put them on for me, please?'

She turned her back while he dropped them round her neck—one, two, three strands—then fastened the tiny catch, his fingers as cold against her skin as the pearls.

When she turned round to show him, he had already taken a step back from her and was looking away towards the jetty. He was going to tell her that it was time to take her home.

The music was still playing quietly, the vibrant tones of 'A Summer Place' filling the aching silence.

'Will you dance with me, Brand?' The words came out of their own volition. 'Just one dance,' she added softly and held out her arms to him.

He frowned, and she thought he was going to refuse. But then, without a word, he took her in his arms, very formally, one hand resting lightly in the small of her back, her left arm on his shoulder, their other hands clasped.

Backwards and forwards they went, the moon above them, the palm trees rustling softly behind them, and the music . . . I shall never, ever forget this moment, Fliss thought, then felt the anguish close tightly like fingers around her throat.

Perhaps Brand felt the little tremor which ran through her, for he drew her nearer to him, then a little nearer still, until gradually, under the hypnotic spell of the music, she surrendered to his arms and they were moving body to body, his arms around her, hers around him, her brow against his chest, his cheek resting on the top of her head.

The music ended and they drew apart, as though waking from a trance. They held each other at arm's length, silver-grey eyes staring into dark sapphire ones, then, at exactly the same moment, each raised a hand to reach towards the other. Brand put his against her shoulder, she laid her palm against his cheek in a soft caress.

Next moment, with an incoherent sound from deep in his throat, he dragged her to him, raining kisses on her upturned face, her eyelids, her throat, with a ferocity which made her knees buckle so that she had to clutch at him for support.

As she cried out, he poured kisses on her shoulders, the upper curves of her breasts, and then dimly she heard the ripping of fabric as he tore her clothes from her, then flung himself out of his own and they were in each other's arms again, their heated skin setting off sparks of electricity as they came together, her breasts crushed against the whorls of dark hair on his chest, her nipples hardening in an ecstasy of wanting and of love. His hand was flat against her lower back, straining her to him so that she felt every powerful surge of that lean, masculine body.

Locked in each other's arms, they crumpled to the warm, welcoming sand. He came down on top of her, shutting out the moon, the stars, the sound of the sea—everything, in the sweet, sensual spell cast over her by the scent of him, the silky feel of his body.

As he entered her, her nails tightened on his shoulders, and a long, shuddering gasp was torn from her. But she sensed him hold himself back, felt him tremble as he struggled to keep himself in check, and moved her hips to deepen his thrusts.

'*No.*' He raised his head and looked blindly at her, his face a dark mask of passion.

'Yes,' she whispered fiercely. 'Yes, Brand.' And at that instant he groaned again and she felt the warmth of his release flood into her. . .

He lay with his cheek against her breast for a long time, then, propping his head on one elbow, gazed down at her.

'I'm so sorry, Fliss.' His voice was heavy with regret. 'I tried to wait for you.'

'Don't be sorry.'

She put her hand over his mouth, and he softly kissed her palm.

'What a generous, giving young woman you are.'

A sombre smile was playing round his lips, but the lovemaking had given him no release; she sensed the tension inside him still, and ached to ease it for him. She gave him a gentle, teasing smile.

'But I was only thanking you for these lovely pearls.'

He lifted one of the strands then let it drop, his eyes wandering slowly down over her body, pale in the moonlight.

'A mermaid,' he murmured huskily. 'A beautiful, warm mermaid. You came from the sea tonight—will you disappear back into the foam at dawn, I wonder?'

'Of course,' she whispered. 'Don't all mermaids?'

'But suppose they can be persuaded to stay? What then?'

'They lose their beautiful fish tails, and then—and then they die.' She shivered as a chill little wind sprang up off the sea.

'You're cold.'

He pulled her to her feet, wrapped her in his shirt, then lifted her in his arms and carried her, her head against his chest, across the beach and into the house. He shouldered open the door and set her down on his bedroom floor, but when he switched on the bedside light she murmured a soft protest and clutched his shirt to her.

'Don't be shy, my sweet.'

His hands were gently lifting her fingers, pulling the shirt away from her, then finally discarding it in a white pool at her feet. She stood, her head bent, as he undid the pearls then removed the pins from her hair, so that it lay spread on her shoulders.

'Don't be shy,' he repeated tenderly as his eyes drank in her graceful curves. 'You have such a beautiful body—pliant, soft. Oh, Fliss,' he put his thumb beneath her chin, turning her face up to his, and at the expression in his eyes she felt her heart flutter wildly like a caged bird, 'if this is a dream, I never want to wake,' he said huskily, then, drawing her to him, he kissed her.

The kiss at first was light and warm, but then, as her lips opened to allow him free access to her mouth, it deepened in intensity, his tongue thrusting into her again and again to taste her sweetness. When at last the kiss ended, she clung to him, her mouth still greedy for him, but he gently held her away.

'No.' He gave her a slow, sensual smile, in which dark fires flickered. 'We have all the time in the world, my sweet.'

Holding her lightly by the shoulders, he kissed her throat, lingering on the pulse at its base until it leapt under his lips, then, as his hands slid slowly down to clasp her arms, his mouth circled one breast, softly and unhurriedly, until it centred on the pulsating nipple and took it in, nipping, sucking at it until it strained towards him.

She closed her eyes, swaying on her heels; her hands flew to grip his shoulders and a throaty gasp of shock-pleasure burst from her. Surely, no sensation could ever be so potent.

But then, Brand's mouth went lower. Holding her by her hips, so that she was imprisoned against his searching lips, he burned a fiery trail across her abdomen, circling, licking around her navel, until she trembled under the strength of desire which pulsated through her, then lower still.

She murmured in feeble protest but he hushed her, holding her inexorably to his mouth as she tried to break free, and gradually this utterly new, wonderful yet frightening sensation gripped her, blotting out every feeling that had gone before. She moved in his arms, her hands tangling in his hair, her nails rasping against his scalp, as her bones turned to fire, her muscles to water.

She wanted him to go on forever, but, as another faint moan came from her throat, he stopped and looked up at her, his eyes taking in her flushed face, her swollen mouth which he had plundered slightly open, her eyes drowning in longing.

Slowly straightening, he picked her up and laid her on his bed. She tried to draw him to her, but he caught both her hands in his, kissing each finger, his lips lingering over the rosy tips, then over each palm and wrist, deliberately soothing her to allow the emotions which had overwhelmed her to ebb just a little.

But then, with his mouth and hands, he drew her almost to that peak again, over and over again, until, dazed by passion and lost to all else except the feel, the smell, the taste of him, she could only cling helplessly to him as he played on her body, tuning it as though it were a musical instrument, to gain the responses he sought from her.

Gradually, with each upward curve of sensation, she felt herself expanding, filling with desire, until her body seemed too tight to be contained within her skin.

'Please.' She breathed a little sigh. 'Please—or I shall die.'

Raising her head, she caught at his nipples with her teeth, until he gave a smothered groan. And at last he moved over her, this time to take full possession of her—very slowly still, drawing for them both every final honeyed drop of sensuous pleasure.

Half fainting, her breathing suspended, she felt herself move in unison with him, oblivious to all beyond the circle of his arms and the ritual dance, as old as time, which they were performing. And then, suddenly, as she clutched at his shoulders, which were wet with sweat, there was release. She did die, shattering into a galaxy of tiny atoms which hung in the air like golden dust, then, as Brand collapsed on her, settled back down to re-form her body—but not the same. Never the same. . .

He rolled off her, opened his eyes, gave her the lazily caressing smile of a replete tiger, put one arm across her and fell instantly into a profound sleep.

Fliss lay, propped on her elbow, watching him for a long time, seeing how the hard lines of his face had all smoothed out, the way he had of holding his mouth compressed quite gone, that tender tiger's sensual half-smile hovering about his lips.

Her heart aching with love, she gazed at him a moment longer, as though she were imprinting him in her mind forever. Then very gently, so as not to disturb him, she drew up the sheet, leaned across to switch off the light, and, curling into him, went to sleep.

She woke with the first pale streaks of dawn from the unshuttered windows across her face. For a moment she stared blankly at the opposite wall, then as, still half asleep, she registered her body, aching and throbbing with delicious languor, she remembered.

Suddenly shy in daylight, she rolled over, taking the sheet with her. But Brand had gone. There were the creases in the sheet where he had slept, the indentation in the pillow where his head had rested. Even, when she put her hand to it, a faint warmth remained—but he was not there.

The bathroom too was silent. He must be preparing breakfast—and yet the thought failed to reassure the prickling unease. Rather stiffly, she got out of bed and, conscious of her nakedness, put on an old black T-shirt of Brand's which lay across a chair.

When she went through to the kitchen, this too was empty and the door to the veranda was half open. As she stood there, that feeling of unease tugging at her mind, she heard a sudden roar and, looking through the trees, could just make out Brand's boat drawing away from the jetty and heading at full speed for the open sea.

She gave a faint smile of relief. How silly she'd been—he must be going out to the reef to catch fish for breakfast. Straining her eyes, she watched until he reached the white line of broken water which marked the inner edge of the reef—and went on past it, with no slackening of speed. She stood perfectly still, until the boat had shrunk to no more than a speck on the horizon.

I never want to wake. . . But he *had* woken from his dream. And now he despised her. Oh, she knew how it must look—that she'd come back to the cay for one reason and one reason only. *Well, that's the truth, isn't it?* an ice-cold voice said silently. '*No!*' She moaned the word aloud and a hard knot of misery formed in her chest. *I came because I love him.*

But perhaps—terror clutched at her—perhaps it was even worse. Had he finally recognised her? Some gesture, some inflection of her voice, the play of moonlight on her body—something at last showing him that the woman he'd held in his arms all night, and the girl at Sombra, were one and the same.

If only she hadn't been so weak as to come back, he'd never have suspected, never have known who she was. If she stayed here now, the contempt in his eyes would flay the skin from her soul. Suddenly terrified that he might be returning, she scanned the horizon, but the boat had quite gone now. All too soon, though, he would come back—but how could she get away?

As her mind hunted desperately for escape, she heard voices coming to her across the water and then, from behind a cluster of palm trees at the far end of the beach, a small boat came into view. Oh, thank heavens—Maybelle's two nephews, on their way home from their night's fishing.

Racing back into Brand's bedroom, she tore open a drawer and dragged out an old pair of denim shorts. She pulled them on then bunched the T-shirt loosely into the waistband. As she closed the drawer, she saw the pearls, still lying on the floor where Brand had dropped them. Even as her heart contracted, she bent and snatched them up, stuffing them into the shorts pocket. In the empty years ahead, they would be her only memory of this bitter-sweet time. . .

She ran headlong to the beach and out on to the jetty. The boat was past the island now, but when she called and waved her arms they saw her and turned back towards the shore. Her spirits shrank from any questions, but mercifully the two men were either too tired or too well-mannered to display the least curiosity.

Seated in the prow, pots of crawfish slung from the side, her feet in a pile of conch shells gleaming silver-pink in the early morning light, she watched as the cay receded to a shadow and the mainland loomed up ahead. Once she glanced fearfully behind her, but this time, she knew, Brand would not pursue her.

Behind the pale mask of her face, her aching brain was busy, over and over again, with the same question: What am I going to do? They were almost at the waterfront before the thought came to her—Go back to England and be an actress. That was it. She'd leave everything behind her and make a fresh start. And this time she'd succeed.

She sat up a little straighter in the boat. I am

Felicia Naughton, she said to herself, then, catching the slightly concerned look in Errol's eyes, smiled reassuringly at him. I am going back to London, and I shall be the greatest actress in the world!

CHAPTER ELEVEN

'MORE flowers, miss.'

The doorman appeared in the entrance of the dressing-room, almost staggering under the weight of an enormous sheaf of pink carnations and rosebuds, trailing pink satin ribbons.

'I'll have those.' And Beaty, her dresser, took the flowers and laid them on the long dressing-table where Fliss was seated.

'Oh, Beaty—they're beautiful.' She touched one pink carnation with a fingertip and bent to take in the heady perfume. 'But who are they from?' She parted the ribbons, but there was no card.

'From the management, most like. Oh, that reminds me—I nearly forgot.'

She took from the pocket of her coat, hanging behind the door, a bag from which she produced a bunch of purple violets and thrust them at Fliss. 'Good luck tonight.'

'Thank you, Beaty. They're lovely.'

She lifted the fragrant flowers to her nose, then suddenly swung round to look at her reflection in the mirror. Her eyes were enormous, darkening with panic until they were the same colour as the violets, and her own deathly pallor showed beneath the pale stage make-up of a little cockney waif.

'Oh, Beaty, I'm frightened. Suppose I'm terrible—suppose the show's a flop?'

'Now, now, you'll spoil your make-up.' The elderly woman took a tissue and gently dabbed at the beads of sweat on Fliss's forehead. 'You'll be great, my duck, I promise you. Look at how it's gone on tour—raving about you, they've been. And then there's all this. . .'

Her gesture took in the flowers, the display of 'Good Luck' cards from Deb and Lizzie, Scott, a beautiful one from her father and stepmother—over the last few months all three of them had, in phone calls and letters to and from New Zealand, moved just a little nearer towards healing that terrible rift—a big smiling black cat from Jim and Sue Bailey—all her friends. Only, there had been nothing from *him*—just an eight-month silence, after he'd vanished from her life that silvery tropical dawn.

'With all these willing you on, you aren't going to blow it,' Beaty went on vehemently. 'You're going to go out there and knock 'em for six.'

The tannoy in the corner crackled. 'Ladies and gentlemen, this is your fifteen-minute call.'

'But I only got the part because Sandie Crane broke her leg.'

'You got the part because the producer knew you could do it.'

'Yes, but——' blind panic was rampaging through her, turning her palms clammy '—I know I was her understudy for the provincial run, but really I was only in the chorus.'

'Her breaking her leg, it was meant,' Beaty intoned

solemnly. 'You can't argue with fate. Now, let's have a look at you.' She subjected Fliss to a searching head-to-toe inspection. 'Hmm. You've got those boots buttoned all wrong, but otherwise you didn't leave much for me to do, did you? What time did you get here?'

Fliss gave her a shamefaced smile. 'Well, I couldn't stay at home, somehow.'

The older woman gave her a knowing wink, then tweaked Fliss's drab rust-black shawl. 'Wanted to see your name in lights, I don't doubt.'

'Well——' She laughed. 'Yes, I did actually.'

Amid the panic, a tiny spurt of elation bubbled softly up at the memory of how, just before slipping in through the stage door, she'd stood in the London side-street, opposite the theatre, drinking in that illuminated sign: 'Opening Tonight—the sensational new musical *Polly Jones*' and, underneath, her own name, 'Felicia Naughton'.

'And don't you worry about that quick change in Act Two. I've put a new zip in your dress, which will make it easier. Now,' she put her hands over Fliss's, 'don't talk any more. You just go into yourself.'

And Fliss sat quietly, letting Beaty fuss unobtrusively around her, adjusting the buttons on her high boots, the lie of the leg-of-mutton sleeves on her blouse, and finally setting on her head the felt hat with its curling ostrich feather.

The tannoy broke the silence. 'Five minutes. Act One, overture and beginners in place, please.' There was a pause. 'And good luck, everybody.'

Fliss stood up stiffly, smiled as Beaty gave her a

brief, careful hug, then walked out of the dressing-room, along the narrow passage and on to the stage, to take her place behind the curtain in the London East-End market scene. . .

Guilt was gnawing at her. Among all the ecstatic celebrations, the inevitable frenetic reactions now the first night was over, she felt remote, alien. At the centre of her personal triumph, where there should be jubilation, there was a numb emptiness, so that for several hours now, as the party surged round her, she'd moved, talked, given endless brilliant smiles, all on automatic pilot.

How she longed for quiet, for bed, but it would be betraying the rest of the cast if she sneaked off before the early editions of the newspapers with the first reviews came out. So she stayed, until her face was stiff, but then, at last, a ragged cheer went up as the doorman appeared with an armful of papers. They were torn from his grasp, people impatiently riffling through them.

'Hey, everybody, listen to this.' It was Dave, the producer. 'Blah, blah—"A wonderful, bitter-sweet, light and dark show. . ." "An exuberant cast who give their all. . ." blah, blah. . . "A century ago, the real Polly Jones burst on the London theatre scene like a brilliant comet, and now Felicia Naughton has done the same. This is the young woman who, just four months ago, was doing a five-minute routine with Dick Whittington's cat in a suburban panto-mime. Now, in true fairy-tale tradition, she has leapt from the back row of the chorus to take the title role of the young cockney music-hall singer who for a short time rivalled the great Marie Lloyd in popularity, before, like an earlier Edith Piaf, she was destroyed by her own emotions." Blah, Blah. . .'

'Here's another one, Fliss.' The actress playing Polly's older sister called across to her. '"Miss Naughton is a genuine discovery. Her portrayal of this wild, tantrum-throwing Victorian girl treads a knife-edge between vitality and anarchy. It would have been very easy for her to go over the top, but with iron self-discipline she keeps a tight grip on the part, and because of that she is able to draw from us much laughter but, among the vibrant songs and dances, aching tears for Polly herself."'

'Congrats, Fliss.' Everyone was gathered round her, generous in their praise, and all at once, as tears stung her eyes, she felt totally overwhelmed.

She edged her way through the jostling crowd but then, as she was about to slip away, she bumped into Dave.

'Congratulations, Fliss.' He wrapped her in an exuberant bear-hug.

'Thank you, Dave—and thanks, for everything. If it hadn't been for you, for your faith in me. . .'

It would have been so easy, after Sandie's accident, for him to have given way to the pressure from the show's main backer, who was demanding that her sudden promotion be only a stopgap and that another star name should be brought in. But Dave had stuck by her, even when the financier had carried out his threat and withdrawn his support, managing to persuade the other, smaller investors to increase their stakes so that the show could make it to the West End.

She kissed his cheek, then slipped out to her dressing-room to pick up her flowers and put on her coat over her simple black jersey dress, then went downstairs, her footsteps echoing on the stone steps.

It was mild outside, the plane trees already breaking into leaf above the raised concrete beds of golden polyanthus and daffodils. She stopped beside one of the beds, fingering the bright yellow trumpets. It was spring—and yet inside her it was still deep winter, as it had been for months. All her success tonight, that everyone had been so happy for, was an empty mockery without the one person she yearned to share it with. Her face screwed up with the old familiar pain then, seeing a taxi cruise down the deserted street towards her, she hailed it.

Letting herself in, she climbed the stairs to the first-floor flat, fumbling in her bag for the keys as she went. Really, how lucky she'd been these last few months. This marvellous acting chance, and, before that, this flat. She'd shrunk from going back to Deb and Lizzie, and had been living in a hostel temporarily when, quite by chance, she'd met Hilary, a few years older than herself, who, as well as trying to make a go of it as a theatrical agent, was looking for someone to share her lovely flat.

She'd offered Fliss the chance to move in and, taking her on her books, had got her her first part, a tiny role in a rep revival of *The King and I*, then the small Christmas pantomime part, and now—this. Yes, she'd been lucky, very lucky. Some people, more talented than she, went all their lives without the break they deserved. So what on earth was she doing, allowing herself to wither slowly away inside?

Tiptoeing in so as not to disturb Hilary, she dropped her coat in the hall and went into the kitchen. She put the flowers on the draining-board, then began to make herself a cup of tea. While the kettle boiled, she walked through to the living-room. It was in darkness. She went across and drew back the curtains then stopped dead, her hand still on the cord.

A man was sitting motionless in the armchair, his back to her. Only his head showed, a thick thatch of black hair.

'Brand?' The sound came out as a guttural croak, as joy and pain surged together inside her.

She moved round to face him and they stared at one another. She wanted to touch him, to see if he was real—in his dark grey suit, white shirt and maroon tie, he looked so different from the last time she'd seen him, and he was so pale, every vestige of his tan completely faded, so that for a moment he really did seem like a ghost. But then the kettle whistled from the kitchen and she said, 'I-I'll make a cup of tea.'

'No.' He leapt to his feet and caught hold of her by the elbows. His hands were warm and solid. 'You look all in. I'll get it.'

He thrust her down on to the sofa and disappeared. When he came back, he set the tray on a low table and squatted down beside it. She watched as he poured out two cups of tea then pushed one towards her.

'H-how did you know?' It was a whisper.

'Where you lived?' He got up then lowered himself on to the sofa alongside her. 'I'm afraid it's confessions time, Fliss.'

'Confessions?' In her lap, her hands were plucking restlessly at each other. 'What do you mean?'

'Well, for a start, Hil is my cousin.'

'What? She can't be.'

'I'm afraid she is. Hilary Carradine Lewis.'

She gaped at him, dawning comprehension making her eyes wide. 'You mean——' she felt for the word '—you *arranged* for her to take me on as her flatmate?'

He nodded.

'But—why?'

He lifted one shoulder in a faint shrug. 'Let's just say, I felt a certain responsibility for you.'

'Oh.' Beneath the shock, anger stirred. 'I suppose you also pulled strings for me to get this part. You could do that, couldn't you?'

'I could,' he admitted. 'But you see, Fliss, I didn't. That's not my way of working.'

'Isn't it?' she said harshly. 'You pull strings, manipulate people whenever and however you want. I'm going to wake your precious cousin and ask her.'

He put his hand on her arm and gently pulled her back down.

'Hil's not here.'

Fliss swung round on him, her eyes blazing. 'You've sent her away—out of her own flat!'

'She's staying with friends, just for tonight.'

'That's exactly what I've been saying. You wanted her out of the way, so without a word she——'

Brand laid one finger on her lips to silence her. 'I needed to talk to you—and it was Hil's idea that she should leave us alone together.'

'Well, you've got your way, so what do you want to say to me?'

But for long seconds he just looked at her, then finally, as she moved restlessly under his gaze, he said, 'You're very pale. What's happened to that lovely tan?'

'The same as to yours, I imagine,' she retorted. But, now that she looked full at him, she saw the shadows beneath his eyes, the lines etched even more deeply around his mouth. 'Oh, Brand,' she said involuntarily, 'you look terrible.'

'Thanks a lot,' he said drily. 'So would you, I imagine, if you'd spent the last six weeks sitting in the back row of the stalls in half the theatres between Bristol and Glasgow.'

'You mean,' she began in a strangled voice, 'you were *there*?'

How hadn't she known? How hadn't—*something* told her that, out there in the warm darkness, was the human being she loved more than anyone else in the world? But then she remembered something else, and her eyes darkened with suspicion again.

'But until the show reached Birmingham, I was only in the chorus.'

He gave her a shadowed smile. 'I know. But I still wanted to see you.'

'Oh,' she said uncertainly, not quite able to meet his eyes. But then, recovering, 'Yes, but when Sandie was hurt, did you honestly not pull——?'

'I swear I pulled no strings for you. The only thing I did was step in with a rescue package when the main backer withdrew and it looked as though the show would fold.'

She gasped. 'But—but that's not what we were told. No one knew that, did they?' she asked fearfully. Had everyone known but her?

'Nobody knew, except Dave and the remaining investors. I insisted on absolute secrecy.' He pulled a wry face. 'I had a funny kind of feeling that *you* just might drop out if you knew I had anything to do with it.'

'But I might have been a disaster. You could have lost your money—and it would have been my fault.' Her voice rose at the appalling thought.

He shook his head. 'I only back winners, Fliss. And I was already quite sure that you'd be one.'

Her brain was still struggling to digest what he had told her. 'So it's all thanks to you that the show went on,' she said slowly. 'And of course, if it weren't for you, I'd never even have thought of musicals. Until you suggested it, out on the cay——' She broke off, trying to fight down the sudden surge of painful memories, then went on, 'But if you've been in England for so long, what about your TV series and the book?'

'Well, they've just had to go on the back burner for a while.'

'But you'll be able to get back to them now.'

'Yes. I'm going back to Jamaica in a couple of days.'

'Oh.' She winced inwardly at the sudden vicious stab of pain, then to try and cover her reaction, she said, 'I-I must go and put my flowers in water.' But before she could stand up, yet another thought had struck her and she sank back. 'You sent me them, didn't you?'

'Yes,' he admitted reluctantly.

'They're beautiful.' She gave him a tremulous smile, then, terrified that her eyes would betray her, turned away again to cradle her cup of lukewarm tea.

'Why did you run away, that morning on the cay?'

The soft words jerked her gaze back to him, to see that old, familiar expression in his eyes that she could never read.

At last she said flatly, 'Because I was afraid you'd despise me.'

'Despise you? Oh, my——' His lips tightened and he went on, 'Fliss how could I possibly despise you when I've spent the last five years despising myself?'

'W-what do you mean?' Sudden fear was paralysing her throat so that she could barely get the words out.

By way of answer, Brand reached for his overcoat, which lay across a chair, and took from the pocket a small box. He held it out to her and she opened it. With unsteady hands, she lifted out the little trinket from its nest of cotton wool.

'So you knew,' she whispered. 'All the time, you knew.'

The tiny amethyst and gold earring, shaped like a

humming-bird, hung from her fingers, quivering slightly.

'That you were the girl at Sombra? Yes.'

'How?' Her voice was barely audible.

'From your birthmark—that funny little heart shape that's always there. What moonlight there was that night showed it up. And then, when I came to see your grandfather——' he was speaking jerkily '—you were going to the beach. Do you remember?'

She nodded, her hair falling forward to screen her face.

'That same birthmark—I saw it again on that lovely young girl as she ran down the steps past me. Well, almost past me.' A shadow of a smile once more. 'And I realised exactly what I'd done. I nearly passed out for a moment—your grandfather was quite worried about me.' She heard the bitter laugh. 'I wonder how he'd have felt if he'd known that just a few nights earlier I'd been making love to his granddaughter—a seventeen-year-old girl.'

'But you weren't to know,' she said softly.

'What kind of excuse is that? Oh, I know that it was all *perfectly legal*,' his voice was savage, 'and at seventeen you already had the body of a woman—a very beautiful woman. But inside you were still a child. I saw that at your grandfather's. He treated you as a child, and that's exactly what you were, a child and——' he paused '—a virgin. You were, weren't you?'

She felt him look at her, but could only nod once more, almost imperceptibly.

He shook his head angrily. 'To take you like that. What an appalling initiation!'

'No, Brand, you mustn't think that!'

'Why not—when it's the truth?' he exclaimed with lacerating self-disgust, then swept on through her protests, 'Even before I knew that, though, I was worried about you. When I came back out to the pool and you'd gone, I chased after you down the drive but then I heard that wretched moped of yours. I didn't know where to start looking for you. In fact,' his lips twisted wryly, 'if I hadn't found your earring by the pool next day, I might even have believed that you were some kind of mirage. And then I did find you—a schoolgirl at your grandfather's.'

He broke off abruptly, but then seemed to be forcing himself to go on, his voice still thick with self-disgust, 'From then on, I tried telling myself that you were every sort of little tart. At Laslo's, then when I found you with that swine Rogers—I think I wanted it to be true to try and assuage my guilt. Then, one day out on the cay, I came up to you on the beach. You'd been arranging a line of shells that you'd collected, and,' his voice changed, taking on a tender, reminiscent quality which made her want to weep, 'you looked up at me with a smile of such shining innocence that I knew I could never delude myself again.'

Fliss set down her cup and took his cold hand between hers. 'But after we'd been diving that day— you sent me away.'

'I know how I hurt you. But I just had to get you off the cay.'

'Why?'

'Because I couldn't trust myself to keep my hands off you any longer, that's why,' he said roughly. 'What a hypocrite I was. To think that your grandfather wanted me, of all people, to be the guardian of your morals. Some guardian!'

She held his hand tight, but he scarcely seemed to notice. 'And then, when you came back on your birthday. . . I'd spent the whole day wrestling with myself—I wanted to go to you so much, but I couldn't. And instead—you came to me.'

'But then, the next morning, you'd gone,' she murmured.

'Suffering from another massive dose of guilt.' He spoke lightly but she sensed the deep self-anger. 'OK, I'd kept my hands off you—just—while you were my ward, but then, on the very night of your birthday. . . When I eventually came back, you'd gone. I spent three days convincing myself it was for the best, then gave in and went over to Jamaica to find you, and found instead that you'd left for London that same day. And so it was too late to tell you the truth.'

'The truth?' Her voice trembled.

'Hil realised straight away. When I rang her and asked her to find you somewhere in London and take you under her wing for me, she laughed and said, "Oh, cousin mine, so you've finally fallen. I'm so glad."'

What was he saying? His words were dancing around in her mind like haphazard pieces of a jigsaw. But then gradually, as her frozen heart began to thaw into life, they came together to make the most beautiful pattern she could ever have imagined.

She turned to him, her face glowing, but he was already getting to his feet, reaching for his overcoat. As he put it on one sleeve caught, and automatically she got up to straighten it for him, then stood as he buttoned himself into it.

At last he turned to her, his face a sombre mask.

'I shall always be grateful to you, Fliss. That time, all those years ago, I was already drifting. I'd come out to Sombra to try to take stock of my life. I was thirty years old, wealthy, totally disenchanted with showbiz—too many Als, too many Laslos. And then, after that night, I really went on the skids. But now— through your loveliness, your innocence, your goodness—and through the feelings that you've awakened in me—you've brought me back to life.'

As she stood, her head bent, he held her gently by the arms and dropped a light, stranger's kiss on her hair.

'After that night at Sombra,' he went on huskily, 'I can't expect you to have any—feelings for me. Oh, don't worry, I'm not going to embarrass you any more,' there was a bitter twist in his voice, 'but, before I go, I want you to know that since then there's been no one else for me. Oh, Fliss,' his fingers suddenly dug into her arms, 'how bloody ironic. I meet the only girl I can ever love, and because of my own brutal behaviour——'

'No—you must never believe that,' she said urgently. Whatever else happened, she wouldn't allow him to go on any longer bearing this dreadful burden of guilt. She swallowed, then went on in a whisper, 'It-it wasn't rape. That night, I-I wanted you to make love to me, Brand.'

'Oh, my sweet Fliss.' His grip tightened convulsively and for one joyous moment she thought he was going to draw her to him, but instead he abruptly released her and smiled sadly down at her. 'But even if you did, you were so young, so very young. . .'

He softly caressed her cheek in a farewell gesture that made her heart ache, then held his hand out to her.

'Goodbye, Fliss.'

'No!' Thrusting it aside, she put her arms around him. His body was as taut as a strung bow, but as she laid her face against the rough cloth she sensed him very slightly begin to tremble.

'Fliss?' He jerked back from her, clasping her by the shoulders so painfully now that she almost cried out.

She raised her head and looked up at him, her eyes radiant with the love which for so long she had struggled to keep hidden deep within herself.

'My darling.' His voice shook.

'Oh, Brand.' She managed a moist smile. 'We've both been so foolish. How we've wasted the last five years. Oh, yes,' she went on as he gazed at her wonderingly, 'I've loved you too, ever since Sombra—and, like you, there's never been anyone else for me.'

'My dear love.' The strain in his face was melting, the lines smoothing away just as they'd done that moonlit night out on the cay, as at last he allowed her joy and love to permeate his own being.

But, as he went to gather her to him, she held him away one moment longer.

'Of course,' she murmured demurely, 'I've signed a six-month contract as Polly——'

'And then there'll be Broadway,' he put in ruefully.

'—but just because we have to wait that long for our honeymoon on your beautiful cay,' she was speaking breathlessly now, as his warm lips, sweet with the promise of love, closed over hers, 'that doesn't mean we have to wait that long for a wedding, does it?'

And with a little sigh of ecstatic happiness she surrendered her mouth, her body, her life to the man who held her tenderly in his arms.

is

 exotic

 dramatic

 sensual

 exciting

 contemporary

 a fast, involving read

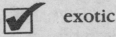 terrific!!

***Harlequin Presents—
passionate romances
around the world!***

"GET AWAY FROM IT ALL" SWEEPSTAKES

HERE'S HOW THE SWEEPSTAKES WORKS

NO PURCHASE NECESSARY

To enter each drawing, complete the appropriate Official Entry Form or a 3" by 5" index card by hand-printing your name, address and phone number and the trip destination that the entry is being submitted for (i.e., Caneel Bay, Canyon Ranch or London and the English Countryside) and mailing it to: Get Away From It All Sweepstakes, P.O. Box 1397, Buffalo, New York 14269-1397.

No responsibility is assumed for lost, late or misdirected mail. Entries must be sent separately with first class postage affixed, and be received by: 4/15/92 for the Caneel Bay Vacation Drawing, 5/15/92 for the Canyon Ranch Vacation Drawing and 6/15/92 for the London and the English Countryside Vacation Drawing. Sweepstakes is open to residents of the U.S. (except Puerto Rico) and Canada, 21 years of age or older as of 5/31/92.

For complete rules send a self-addressed, stamped (WA residents need not affix return postage) envelope to: Get Away From It All Sweepstakes, P.O. Box 4892, Blair, NE 68009.

© 1992 HARLEQUIN ENTERPRISES LTD.   SWP-RLS

"GET AWAY FROM IT ALL" SWEEPSTAKES

HERE'S HOW THE SWEEPSTAKES WORKS

NO PURCHASE NECESSARY

To enter each drawing, complete the appropriate Official Entry Form or a 3" by 5" index card by hand-printing your name, address and phone number and the trip destination that the entry is being submitted for (i.e., Caneel Bay, Canyon Ranch or London and the English Countryside) and mailing it to: Get Away From It All Sweepstakes, P.O. Box 1397, Buffalo, New York 14269-1397.

No responsibility is assumed for lost, late or misdirected mail. Entries must be sent separately with first class postage affixed, and be received by: 4/15/92 for the Caneel Bay Vacation Drawing, 5/15/92 for the Canyon Ranch Vacation Drawing and 6/15/92 for the London and the English Countryside Vacation Drawing. Sweepstakes is open to residents of the U.S. (except Puerto Rico) and Canada, 21 years of age or older as of 5/31/92.

For complete rules send a self-addressed, stamped (WA residents need not affix return postage) envelope to: Get Away From It All Sweepstakes, P.O. Box 4892, Blair, NE 68009.

© 1992 HARLEQUIN ENTERPRISES LTD.   SWP-RLS

"GET AWAY FROM IT ALL"

Brand-new Subscribers-Only Sweepstakes

OFFICIAL ENTRY FORM

This entry must be received by: June 15, 1992
This month's winner will be notified by: June 30, 1992
Trip must be taken between: July 31, 1992—July 31, 1993

YES, I want to win the vacation for two to England. I understand the prize includes round-trip airfare and the two additional prizes revealed in the BONUS PRIZES insert.

Name _____

Address _____

City _____

State/Prov. _____ Zip/Postal Code _____

Daytime phone number _____
(Area Code)

Return entries with invoice in envelope provided. Each book in this shipment has two entry coupons — and the more coupons you enter, the better your chances of winning!
© 1992 HARLEQUIN ENTERPRISES LTD. .   3M-CPN

"GET AWAY FROM IT ALL"

Brand-new Subscribers-Only Sweepstakes

OFFICIAL ENTRY FORM

This entry must be received by: June 15, 1992
This month's winner will be notified by: June 30, 1992
Trip must be taken between: July 31, 1992—July 31, 1993

YES, I want to win the vacation for two to England. I understand the prize includes round-trip airfare and the two additional prizes revealed in the BONUS PRIZES insert.

Name _____

Address _____

City _____

State/Prov. _____ Zip/Postal Code _____

Daytime phone number _____
(Area Code)

Return entries with invoice in envelope provided. Each book in this shipment has two entry coupons — and the more coupons you enter, the better your chances of winning!
© 1992 HARLEQUIN ENTERPRISES LTD.   3M-CPN